CONTENTS

Chemistry

when it's lust at first sight

Tiye Love

WWW.TIYELOVEBOOKS.COM

Chemistry

She was his sexy college professor.

He was her hot student.

Like two magnets, their attraction was undeniable...

Destined for marriage has always been Simone Austin's belief and now that her career is where she wants it, she is ready for forever. In walks one sexy, Chris Alexander, apologetically late to her class and from the first moment their eyes met, he tempts her to forget her careful approach to love and focus on their tantalizing moments of the here and now...

Chemistry by Tiye Love

ASIN: B07RHV4VNM

The meeting of two personalities is like the contact of two chemical substances: If there is any reaction, both are transformed. - Carl Jung

Chapter 1: Teacher's Pet

He was the very definition of Chemistry, the moment he walked in my class.

I was excited about my second year of teaching. I was no longer the novice or unsure of how to deal with difficult or entitled students. This year would be easier, and I would be able to get serious about my research, so I can focus on earning tenure. I had already met my teaching assistant and she was hyped about working with me, a definite change from my last TA who shirked his duties every chance he got. I was relaxed and ready for my students this year. Those were my thoughts as I walked into my Monday morning class that thankfully began at ten. Last semester, this class started at eight and I barely made it through morning traffic and parking. Yep, my teaching schedule was even better this year. This was an advanced course, so I only had thirty-one students as opposed to my other three intro classes which easily had way over one hundred students. All in all, a good way to start off the semester.

I wore black slacks and a black button up blouse with a jean jacket, professional but casual. I had decided to cut my long hair into an inverted bob, still long enough to wear the occasional ponytail or bun when I wanted a different look. I felt confident as I walked in and went straight to my table in the front and heard a few surprised gasps. I know must students probably thought I was one of them because at twenty-eight I probably appeared more like twenty - one reason I cut my hair hoping to age myself just a little.

I got my notes together, set up my power point which gave class details, regarding my name, course title, course syllabus location, and office hours. This allowed my class time to wander in and get settled since this was only the first day. There was the usual nervous energy of the first day of a new semester, especially in the fall. Although I had only been at LSU a year, I already preferred spring semester. Everyone seemed more chill during that time of year and we had spring break.

A couple of students approached me on whether they were in the appropriate class and if I could add them since the class was now officially closed. I was so busy addressing their concerns, time flew by and when I checked my watch class was supposed to begin ten minutes ago. I looked around and everyone seemed ready for me to begin and I took a breath, "Welcome to Organic Chemistry, I'm Dr. Simone Austin and if you're here today, I promise you will be a different person than when you leave my class because you will have learned something new. Even if all you can say at the end of the semester is, 'I learned my professor's name'." I heard a few snickers and I got my desired response.

Their open laughter helped me relax and shed the nervous jitters. I walked back and forth in front of them as I explained my course. "Chemistry is a part of our daily life. It makes up how we think, move, and even feel."

I walked to the door and closed it before continuing my spiel. "Chemistry is important...

The door opened interrupting my thought, and in walked one of the handsomest men I had even seen. He looked apologetic the moment he came through the door. "Sorry...I got lost."

"It's fine," I said hoping my voice didn't betray my instant attraction at the sound of his deep voice and his appreciative glance when I raised my eyes to his. "Welcome."

He then smiled, and my stomach clenched. I was always a sucker for men whose face could light up with a smile. *Down, girl, he is a student.* I stood slightly back as he crossed in front of me searching for a seat. He even smelled good. I made myself look away from him and quickly identified a seat for him.

"There's a seat over there." I pointed. It was next to a blonde who looked more than happy that he would be sitting next to her. I didn't blame her, though I wished I found another seat first, preferably next to the football player, proudly wearing his jersey, who sat just two rows behind. All eyes followed him as he smiled at the blonde and took a seat. I returned my attention to the class. "As I was saying we see Chemistry in our everyday lives. Raise your hand if you ever heard the term that someone is 'chemically imbalanced'?"

Most hands went up including the handsome student whose gaze was intense as I stood before the class. "Does anyone really know what that means?" There was no response from the class which I expected.

"I've heard it in relation to Bipolar," the late student spoke once again drawing attention to himself.

"Yes, but what does it mean?" I spoke directly to him but made sure to address the class.

"I think it means that for people who have Bipolar, the chemicals in the brain don't work as they should." He answered again.

I smiled liking that he was willing to talk on the first day. My male students rarely spoke, especially Black men. "Your name?"

"I'm not sure what you call it...oh, you mean my name." He grimaced at his mistake before giving me a slow half-smile. "It's Chris."

"I call students by their last name." I leaned against the table with my legs crossed and hands resting on the table on either side of me. I might have appeared calm, but I got hot at this simple exchange between the two of us. I was torn with continuing this conversation or changing the subject in hopes of engaging another student.

He corrected. "Chris Alexander."

Great, even his name was sexy to me. *Focus.* "Well, Mr. Alexander, you're right. In the simplest explanation, the chemicals in our brains are causing us to be 'crazy.' And please no offense if you have or have a loved one with Bipolar. I'm just making a point. Besides all of us have a little crazy in us whether we're ever labeled as Bipolar or some other mental health diagnosis because of the chemicals in our brain. Let's call them neurotransmitters. And when our transmitters are influenced by our lives like stress, poor diet, lack of sleep, chaotic environment and genetics, then we all behave differently."

This time Mr. Alexander raised his hand. "What about love? Is that included when we talk about chemistry?" There were a few 'oohs' and 'good question' from the other students.

I was glad I leaned against the table at his question or I may have tripped, not because of the question but because of his amused look when he asked. I folded my arms and raised an eyebrow as I returned his gaze. "Yes, you have to have chemistry in order to have love." Once again, the class made pleased comments and had more questions. "Look, look it's much more complicated and we have a whole semester to explore that question and more. But thank you, Mr. Alexander, for jumping right in. It makes the class more fun and time go faster if there is participation."

"No problem. I hate boring classes and so far, I can tell this won't be one of them," he responded.

"Dude, you already trying to be teacher's pet'?" Another of my male students spoke from the back of the room in jest. And once again everyone laughed.

"I don't mind that title at all," Chris...I mean Mr. Alexander calmly responded and there were a few more 'ooh's'.

"Hey, I show no favoritisms. You ask questions, get involved in discussion and your grades usually reflect that involvement. And I do my best because I hate boring classes too." My legs were not yet strong enough for me to walk without tripping, so I continued to lean against the table. "You can find my syllabus online. If you have any trouble, feel free to email me. I'm open and available to my students. There is no dumb answer or question though I may look as if you did respond in that way. Sorry, I can't help my face." Some students laughed. "Please, pay no attention to my very expressive face. Seriously, I love chemistry and think it's the simplest thing in the world and then reality hits that this subject can be difficult for a lot of people. I realize that most people see this course as intimidating and I will do my best to make it relatable to each of you, so please get comfortable in this class and ask away. You will pass this class if you put forth effort. The only students who fail are those who do not show up for class, who miss exams and assignments."

I found myself nervous as I did my usual spiel about my style of teaching, because I could feel his energy. "You know since it's just the first day, we'll wrap up early and I'll see you on Wednesday. Follow the syllabus and be ready for next class. I love pop quizzes, by the way." This time there were the expected groans.

As the class began to pile out shortly after, I began to gather my belongings and I heard his voice behind me. "Hey...Dr. Austin, right?"

"Yes." I turned around and automatically placed my notepad in front of my chest. He glanced at my protective stance for a moment before returning to my face.

"I wanted to apologize again. I'm normally not late, especially for my advanced courses. Just wanted to check in and make sure I didn't miss anything," he said giving me direct eye contact. I willed myself to return his gaze unaffected, which is what I would do for any student. But damn if he didn't have the prettiest dark brown eyes. "I hope you didn't mind that I asked you that question. I was just curious what you thought."

"I mean it when I say there are no dumb questions. I hope you keep speaking in class. It was refreshing." Focus on his eyes and not his full lips surrounded by a well-groomed mustache and connecting goatee.

"Cool...you never answered my question." He bit his lip as if he read my mind.

"I...told you..." I said flustered. "We'll discuss that question and others later in the semester."

"No, I meant did I miss anything because I was late?" He frowned slightly.

"Um...no." I had to mentally shake my head and get it together before he could tell my attraction. "I'd just started when you walked in. You are fine...I mean you're good." I stumbled over my words when I realized I had been thinking how freaking fine he was when I voiced it.

"Okay. I look forward to your class. Like I said earlier, I can already tell I'm going to enjoy it." He had a slight smug grin. Great. He probably read my thoughts. "Can I help you with anything?" He gestured to my notes and laptop.

"No...no. I got it. See you on Wednesday." I grabbed my bag and stuffed my papers in it. My bag was a mess, but I was trying to get out of here. We were now alone, and he made me nervous. The kind of nervous when a girl is talking to the boy, who she is crushing on but can never have. "I just need to get my pen..." I looked around for my favorite pen.

"You mean this one?" Chris moved closer and I was helpless to move away as his muscled arm reached slightly above me to remove my pen from my hair. I took the pen from him, careful not to touch his hand, knowing instinctively I would feel sparks. "Thank you. Nice to meet you Mr. Alexander," I said hoping he took the hint to leave before things got out of control, like my own self-control.

"Likewise." He nodded while assessing me and then he turned and headed to the door. "See you in class, Dr. Austin."

My gaze followed him as he left the room and I leaned against the table, even more thrilled about this semester, if he was any indication. Chris Alexander would be a fun student to teach. He was already involved and not afraid to ask questions. I would just have to keep reminding myself that I am only *teaching* him chemistry.

Chapter 2 : The Encounter

It was finally the end of the semester and students were hounding me about grades, extra credits, and make-up exams. I graded papers, hoping I didn't have any more students during my office hours. God, I hated this time of year. My only saving grace was that I had Christmas break and would be spending spend time with Derek, the new guy I met at my cousin's home at Thanksgiving. We met for coffee over the weekend and we had a little "chemistry" and we had talked a couple of times since then.

I hadn't had a date or sex in a while and hoped I could kill two birds in one stone with Derek. We were attracted to each other and we both wanted to be in a relationship. I smiled thinking of spending time in the company of a nice-looking man. That would be so good right about now. Ever since I became an Assistant Professor, at twenty-seven last year, my dating life had been non-existent. I don't know if I intimidated or if men were threatened that I had a doctorate in chemistry. As a lowly broke graduate student, I had plenty of dates that went nowhere. With a PhD I had not had much luck with dating until Derek. We seemed to hit it off and I looked forward to the holidays with him. Especially if dating another man meant I would finally stop obsessing about my student.

I had to stop saying his name in my thoughts and would constantly remind myself that he was my student. He had been a hit and always had the ladies in the class hanging on to his every word, including myself, truth be told. Although he made my class the best I've had thus far, I was also glad that it was over before I made a fool over myself and succumbed to my fantasies.

Suddenly, I heard a knock on my opened door interrupting my thoughts and I looked up and saw him. My stomach fluttered, and I touched it as if he could tell. "Yes?"

Chris...I mean Mr. Alexander remained silent and walked into my office and closed the door.

"Please keep the door open," I said hoping I sounded stern and not breathless. I had managed to go a whole semester without making a fool of myself over him. *Why or why is he here now and we are utterly alone?*

"What I have to say is private," he countered in his deep voice sending chills up my spine. He sat across from me, legs slightly open, confident, without waiting for a response. I looked at the closed door feeling the need to stand and open it back before I did something stupid. In these close quarters, the subtle attraction between us became palpable. I should just get up and open the door myself. Instead my legs betrayed me, and I remain seated, curious, wondering what he needed to say to me.

The front of my desk was pushed against the wall and I would simply turn in my chair to speak to my students. I didn't like the formality and barrier that talking from behind a desk created. Today, I found myself wishing we did have something between us. I wasn't sure how to identify this electricity that I'd never felt before for any other man. It had existed between us since he walked into my class late on the first day and apologized with a smile for his lateness. And true to his word, he never missed a day or had been late again. He'd sat in the same seat, next to the blonde student, whose name I now know is Amber. His piercing glance made every word I spoke important. And he always participated in class discussions in a way that made the class more interesting not just for me, but the class as well. We all waited to see what Chris would ask or say, which was usually more insight to what I discussed. Although I loved his participation, an undercurrent of attraction lingered between us that I hoped wasn't noticeable to the rest of the class.

Other professors informed me that students would often develop crushes on us and to not get caught up since we were all adults. Since I taught two advance level classes each semester, many of my students were only a few years younger than me and even had a few who were older. I didn't know Chris's age at first and assumed he was older because he seemed more mature than the other students based on the questions he would ask and that he aced every quiz or test. I later discovered he was twenty-six when I looked through student files.

I don't know why I couldn't get him out of my mind. Besides the first day, we never were alone again. Initially, I would linger after class, hoping he would approach me again, but inevitably some female student would grab his attention and either I or he would leave first. As the semester progressed, I dressed for him and wore more make-up than usual. When Chris never asked to see me after class or attended any study groups, I thought maybe he didn't have the crush and it was all me. That maybe I was projecting my attraction onto him. Once I made that self-discovery, I changed my classroom attire and would rush out as soon as class was over. I'd made sure my door remained open, just in case he needed to see me during office hours. He had never visited me until now.

"So how can I help you, Mr. Alexander?" I decided to pretend that the energy in the room was normal. I put a pen in my bun and crossed my legs hating that I wore a dress because he slowly looked at my legs before he met my eyes. Although uncomfortable, I was determined to treat him like all my other students and not as a grown man who I found sexy as hell. "You said it was a private manner?"

"Yes." He leaned closer. "I find you extremely attractive."

I lost my breath not expecting him to address the large elephant in the room. "Excuse me?"

"I'm having difficulty studying for your final because all I do is think about you." He gazed into my eyes. "The way you walk, you talk, the excitement you get when you're teaching. I find all of it and you hot."

"Um...sometimes...it is normal for students...to have crushes." I played with the pen in my hair, nervous because I had been having trouble focusing on my work because of the man sitting in front of me. Maybe after a few dates and sex with Derek, I would stop feening for my off-limits student.

"I'm a grown man and I know what it means to have a crush." He touched my knee and I jerked unconsciously, and he kept his hand there daring me to move it. "I can't stop thinking about how much I want to fuck you."

I gasped aloud not believing he had the balls to tell me in such plain terms what he wanted to do to me. Honestly, I didn't know whether to be upset or wet. He was after all one sexy man and I'm a young college professor, not blind. Fortunately, reason and sanity took over and I put my hand firmly on his to remove it from my knee. "You're being so inappropriate, and I need you to leave now."

He quickly took my hand and pulled me slightly toward him. "Is it inappropriate because you're my teacher or what I said? I'm sorry if I offended you, but it's how I feel. You have been driving me crazy this whole semester and I can't stop thinking about how much I want to fuck you, make love, have sex or whatever you want me to call it. I just know I want to be inside of you like yesterday."

I tried to pull my hand back because my panties were now moist, and I was weakening. He loosened his grip but did not let go. "Let my hand go, please." I sighed when he continued to hold my hand. "It doesn't matter, it's all inappropriate. You can't say these things to me."

"Why not? I'm telling you exactly what I want. Now, it's your turn to be real with me. If you saw me out at a restaurant or a bar, and I approached you, you would have given me your number. And you would have spent the night with me that first night. I can tell you feel something for me, or I wouldn't still be holding your hand," he implored.

I then took a breath and a chance by giving him direct eye contact because he was right. I would have never turned him down outside of this situation. He was too freaking hot and the chemistry too strong to ignore. "You're not wrong I'm attracted to you, but I am your professor. I can lose my job and... and I need you to leave. I'll forget we had this conversation and chalk it up to a mutual crush." I rose to get him to do the same, so I could get him far, far away from me. But when he stood, only inches from me, I swooned. He caught the top of my arms, looked at me, and before I could protest, captured my lips with his rather full ones.

The minute Chris opened my mouth with his tongue, I lost whatever inhibitions that prevented me from acting on this fantasy I had envisioned from the very first day. I kissed him back with all the pent-up passion I had for him over the last few months. He pushed me backwards until my ass touched my desk. He placed my arms around his neck and began rubbing my breasts through my silk dress as he continued to kiss me. Both nipples hardened when he lowered his head to suck on my left nipple through my dress. I wanted desperately to feel his lips against my skin. He must have read my mind because he unbuttoned the top of my dress and unsnapped the front clasp freeing my breasts. His appreciative glance and accompanying moan emboldened me to reach down and touch his hard, big dick through his jeans.

"Why are you so fucking sexy?" He whispered in my ear as he moved against my hand. "Do you know how many times I wanted to fuck you in the classroom? To bend you over the table that you like to lean against as you teach and fuck you senseless."

"Hmmm and I wanted you to." I had never been turned on so much in my life because all I craved at that moment was to feel him inside of me. Without another thought, I sat on my desk and opened my legs to him. I lifted his sweater off him revealing a chest that could be photographed for any magazine. He was much finer than I had imagined, and I kept running my hands up and down his chiseled torso in wonder. "I didn't realize your shirts were hiding all of this. When do you have time to work out?"

Chris gave me a pleased smile and reached in his back pocket for his wallet. He pulled a gold wrapper out and opened it. I then unbuckled his belt and unbuttoned his jeans as he quickly finished the job by pushing them and his boxer briefs down at the same time. He was also much larger than I thought he would be, but I knew whatever he gave, I could take. He rolled the condom on with one hand as he kissed me again. He then quickly, moved my panties to the side and entered me with a powerful thrust. I held on to his neck tight as he pounded into me driving me insane with his moves. He was easily the best I ever had, and he had only been inside me for a few seconds. I knew my orgasm would be fucking amazing and though what we were doing was taboo, there was no way, this would be our last time. As I tightened my legs around his waist, I marveled at how everything happened so fast, that we would end up doing this within seconds of being alone.

I moaned in encouragement as my glance fell on my door. I closed my eyes when I noticed that he had locked my door when he walked in, knowing that we would end up having sex. The thought alone that he knew he could have me, spurred me on and I licked his ear before pulling his lobe in my mouth. He put his hands around my hips and smashed into me over and over until we both panted the sexy sounds of an orgasm.

As we came within seconds of each other, he kissed me to drown out my loud moans of pleasure. My arms were still clasp around his neck as I regained my senses. He pulled out of me and I felt like a part of me was already missing, he grinned. "That was much better than any of my fantasies."

"Mine too," I admitted before I realized it causing him to grin even harder. "I mean...I... this should not have happened."

"Too late. We did it and we both enjoyed it." He began to kiss me again.

I almost succumbed again to his sweet, sweet lips before I pushed him away. "Chris, please stop."

He looked at me as he pulled up his underwear and jeans. "My name sounds good on your tongue. I was wondering if you remembered my first name." In class, I was more formal and always called him by his last name.

"Of course, I remember your name." I took a breath to calm my nerves as he suddenly lifted me off my desk to stand on my feet. I cleared my throat and began, "I mean Mr. Alexander, I apologize. I should know better than to have..." I could feel beads of sweat on my forehead just thinking of what I had just done with my student that I had always called Chris only in my head when he was just a fantasy. "I don't know what just happened..."

"Dr. Austin, or should I say Simone, we just had hot sex," he said calmly as he gave me my panties and picked up his sweater.

"I prefer Dr. Austin." I practically snatched and put them back on quickly and snapped the front clasp of my bra. "I know that...I meant I don't know what would make me act like that."

He put on his sweater covering his damn near perfect chest and finished buckling his belt still watching me. "It's not complicated. You wanted me as much as I wanted you. It happens."

I took a step back to lean on my desk for support at his words. His presence, still so overwhelming, I had to study my shoes to avoid direct eye contact. "I could lose my job. We can't talk about this anymore. I had a lapse in judgement. It can't happen again. Please say you understand."

"Of course, I understand why you're worried." Chris buttoned my dress sending sparks all over my body. "There's no need. I won't say anything to anyone. Besides, I was the aggressor. I came in here ready to tell you how I feel. I thought I would just ask you out and maybe even kiss you now that the semester is almost over. I didn't expect to have sex. I would apologize but why would I say sorry for an experience that we both wanted and that I'll always remember?"

I removed his hand, and moved closer to the door, knowing that I would worry because what I did was unacceptable. "Well, I was wrong, and I really think you need to leave."

"It's cool, relax, Sim... Dr. Austin. We are both grown. It's not like I'm in high school and you took advantage of me. You look like a student yourself so you can't be that much older than me. If anything, I took advantage of you. I did come in here and tell you what I wanted and kissed you first."

After being reminded of the truth, I became angry, more because of the inner turmoil he caused. "You know what... you're right. You locked my door. You came here to do only one thing and I can't believe I let you do it." I glared at him when I thought about the fact that he locked my door.

Chris frowned. "Now, you're going to play the victim. I didn't realize I locked your door, I only closed it because I didn't want anyone else to hear what I wanted to say to you. Honestly, all I hoped for was that you felt the same and maybe we would go out on a date, maybe even a kiss, but you opened your legs for me." He stepped back and reasoned, "I get you scared but you have to admit that what we shared was hot and we really vibe."

I had to end this conversation before I let my body rule my head, so I unlocked the door and opened it. One of my female students walked up to my door. I glanced back belatedly at Chris to see if he was fully dressed and then turned back to my student. I felt his stare. "I'm sorry, I can't meet. I'm leaving for the day for an emergency."

"But, Dr. Austin...I have a question about the final." She looked past me at Chris and smiled flirtatiously, which struck a jealous nerve. I had to get a grip, she could flirt all day with him, I couldn't.

"Email me and I promise you I'll answer any questions. I really have to go." I tried to act nonchalant when Chris touched my back as he moved past me without another word and walked down the hall. I had to fight the urge to follow him. "He was my last student today."

"It's just a quick question." She had the nerve to turn her head to watch him though she spoke to me. Thankfully she was too caught into his swag to pay attention to the fact that we probably looked like we just finished having sex. I know my face had to be flushed and my office reeked of sex.

"I can't, Ms. Fredericks. Email me, please." I nodded before stepping back inside and closing the door, not caring if I seemed rude. I sunk in my chair still in disbelief about what just happened with one Mr. Chris Alexander. I looked at my watch, everything had transpired in the last thirty minutes. I just had sex with one of my students and though it was wrong on so many levels, God, help me, I wanted to do him again and again.

Chapter 3: Once more and we are done

I couldn't sleep the next two days with vacillating thoughts of how amazing Chris felt inside of me and fearing repercussions if anyone found out. He was so freaking fine, and I had never had a sexual experience like that in my life. Maybe because it happened so suddenly or because he had been a daydream come true. All I know is I have been wet since he touched me on my back on his way out of my office. I'm not sure why I completely forgot myself and let a man I barely knew fuck me like that. Okay, I knew a little about him, so he wasn't a complete stranger. He was intelligent, and older than my typical students. He could banter with me as he did often in class when we would have discussions, so I knew he had good conversation. Chris took his education seriously based on the grades he earned in my class and he really seemed to be a good guy. I had hoped my crush wasn't noticeable during those exchanges. Given how certain he was that he could be so candid with me in my office, that was highly unlikely.

I stared at the ceiling in bed, the night before the final exam, nervous and excited about seeing Chris again. Would he act like nothing happened between us and more importantly how did I want him to react? Every time I had sex with a man, I viewed him differently, even if I had no expectations. I couldn't help it, but once a man was naked against my skin and inside of me, I was automatically closer to that man. Just thinking of how Chris looked at me with such need right before he kissed me, made me want to touch myself wishing he was in between my legs with his tongue inside of me. I had grown very accustomed to masturbation in the past year and after having the real thing, my fingers weren't cutting it. Just thinking of his sensuous kiss and his hard chest against my soft breasts...Fuck, I wanted him even more since I had a taste. But as much as I want to ignore what's right, I couldn't.

Outside of my mad attraction to him, I honestly loved teaching him. Students like him, were the reason I didn't take a job paying twice my salary at a makeup company in New York. I wanted to teach and make a difference in people's lives. And messing around with a student would be a certain end to my teaching career.

I didn't tell anyone, not even Bea who had been my best friend forever. She would say if I wasn't horny, I wouldn't have been tempted by my student. She constantly criticized my dating life or lack thereof. She was into online dating and had made a pledge to go on at least three dates a month for the past year, which she accomplished. Although she wanted to be married like me, she wasn't trying to find a husband. She wanted to date like a man and see how it felt to have options. It did sound like fun without the worry of whether the guy wanted commitment. However, she lived in Washington, DC, where we were from and had many more options than I did here in Baton Rouge. I was also too scared to do online dating and end up with one of my students. So, I went to sleep sexually frustrated though I was resolved to let that sexy interlude be a wild memory and remain polite but professional when I saw him. I needed to focus on my upcoming date on Saturday. It was my first real one since I moved here and maybe, just maybe Derek would help me forget one handsome and fine as fuck, Chris Alexander.

After a restless night, exhausted I arrived at class to administer the final exam unsure of how he would behave toward me when we saw each other again. I grew worried after thirty minutes into the exam and he still hadn't arrived. What if he couldn't face me? Or was he angry because I treated him like the consensual sex was one-sided? I fretted as I sat at my desk waiting for each of my students to finish their exams. I had my laptop with me, and I looked up student files to get his number. I didn't want him to fail his final because he avoided me. I could barely wait for my last student to turn in their exam before I made a mad dash to my office, to call him.

"Hello." His deep voice soaked my panties.

"Hi, is this Mr. Alexander?" I had it bad already. "Um...this is Dr. Austin...I -"

"I know your voice." He interrupted. "Is there a reason you're calling?"

"Your exam...you had Finals today."

"I didn't feel ready for it...I couldn't focus while I tried to study. I think you know why."

"You can't just *not* take the final. You have an 'A' in the course, it will bring you to a C."

"I'm okay with a C. If that's all, I enjoyed your class. Take care." He sounded annoyed.

"Chris...please," I said without thought, suddenly afraid that this would be our last conversation.

"Yes?" I could hear the smile in his voice.

"Please don't let what happened between us affect your grade. You didn't do anything I didn't want, alright? I admit I like you, and I let my emotions rule my common sense. But you're one of my favorite students because you get Chemistry and I already feel guilty enough about what we did. I don't need to know I also contributed to you getting a lower grade then you deserve. I have make-ups on Saturday in the lab for noon. I expect to see you, okay?" I asked quietly.

"Okay," he responded just as soft.

∞∞∞∞

On Saturday, Chris and three other students were already in the lab waiting to take their finals. I gave each of them their exams individually while they remained seated. When I gave him his exam, he touched my hand purposely and looked up at me with a serious expression. I gave him a subtle nod glad that he decided to take his exam, ignoring the intense feelings he invoked, before heading back to the front where I planned to sit and grade exams.

As each student left one by one, my stomach churned in anticipation of being alone with him again. I wanted to go to him and then I wanted to get the hell out of dodge. Damn, I wished I met him outside of here. I love sex, usually in the parameters of a relationship. However, based on my deep attraction to Chris, I would be content if all we ever did was fuck. But I met him while he was a student in my class. And no dick is worth my job.

Once the last student turned in his exam, I gathered my paperwork, preparing to leave as soon Chris turned in his test. Resolve made to not get pulled back into his orbit.

"What are you doing after this?" He spoke from his seat.

I tapped my foot in mild frustration that I had to quell the desire to be with him. "I don't thin -"

"You're not my teacher anymore. What are you doing after this?" Chris asked again as he got up with his exam.

I warily watched him approach me unsure if I could fight temptation. Today, he wore dark blue sweats with a coordinating hoodie. I don't recall that he ever wore sweats. He was usually dressed casually when he came to class. Not that he wasn't neat and groomed in his sweats. The fabric unfortunately clearly outlined his package. Chris passed me his exam. Because I was sitting, his crotch was eye level and I couldn't seem to look away.

"My eyes are up here." He had a slight smile.

I didn't respond and placed my papers and then computer in my bag.

"Seriously, are you done after this? There's this restaurant I think you would love..."

"It doesn't matter what I'm doing it won't be with you," I snapped. I had a hard time resisting his offer and this damn sexual energy.

Chris put his hands up and backed from me. "You know what? I thought you were cool, but I guess I was wrong. I can take the hint before I'm accused of harassment. Probably best I walk away."

I stood quickly and came around the table, not wanting him to leave thinking I thought poorly of him or he had the wrong impression of me. "Wait, I'm sorry...I'm usually not like this and if things were different, well..."

"What would happen if things were different?" He moved to stand so close to me, I had to bend my head back to see his face.

"I'm still a professor at this university, and this isn't a big city. Nothing can come from what we did the other day."

He placed his hand lightly on my waist like I was already his woman. "I asked you what would be different?"

"You *know* what would be different." I gazed up into his eyes and bit the corner of my lip.

"Touch me." Chris tightened his hold on my waist.

"Not a good idea." I felt lightheaded.

He took the pen out of my hand and moved my hand to inside his sweats. He guided my hand over his now fully erect dick and closed my hand around him. I know I should be stopping him, but I was entranced with his boldness.

When he began to move my hand, I reminded him. "Anyone could walk in here."

"True, but it's Saturday and a make-up day and most people are already gone on break. There are no windows and the doors lock automatically once closed. No one can see us." His mouth opened slightly in pleasure as he continued to give himself a hand job with my hand. "I told you the other day in the office what I wanted to do to you in here."

I quickly imagined the scenario and grew even wetter in anticipation before common sense prevailed. I attempted to pull my hand away, but he held on. "Let my hand go, Mr. Alexander."

"Only if you call me Chris. I'm not in your class anymore."

"Look, Chris..."

He then turned me around so that my back was flush against his front as he placed his arms around me and began kissing my neck. "I noticed that you wore a dress. You wanted this to happen again. You wanted it to be easy for me to do this," he said as he went under my dress, pulled down my tights, and rubbed my very slick clit slowly. "It's why I wore these sweats with no underwear knowing you didn't just call concerned about my grade. You wanted to see me again. You wanted me to fuck you again."

"Fuck you," I cursed him, and I covered his hand inside my panties trying to control his movements to no avail.

"If that's what you want…" He moved my head to the side so he could tongue me. His tongue…damn, his tongue. *Why did he have to know how to kiss so well?*

"You win…just please fuck me," I said as I pushed my stuff out of the way and bent over on the table, unable to deny him any longer and uncaring of the consequences.

I heard the condom wrapper seconds before he entered me with a hard thrust. I hit the table with my palm as he fucked me. "Shit, you feel so good."

"No, Simone, your pussy is good," he whispered in my ear, the sound of my name on his lips made me arch my back more. "Yeah…baby give it to me. Fuck…fuck…"

I spread my hands on either side of the table and gave in to the delicious feel of his dick inside of me. He was right he wasn't my student anymore and after today, I wouldn't see him anymore. He wasn't a chemistry major. I might as well as get fucked well while I could.

Chris used my lower back as his leverage to fuck me deep and slow. I closed my eyes savoring the sinful pleasure of his rhythmic hip action in such a public place. A place where I taught for the past year and would never look at the same again because of the man inside of me right now. A man with whom I had no attachment, no commitment, and now no guilt. Just sex between two consenting adults, I crooned, "Ooh, I wish you could fuck me all the time. Your dick is so freaking amazing."

"That could be arranged," he said as his pace increased until we were both desperately wanting sweet, sweet release. And when it came for both of us, we were loud. He fell on top of me laughing. "Let's hope no one heard us either."

His easy laughter made me long for something more and I reached behind me to hug him before I tapped his neck, so he could let me up. Again, once he left my body, I felt like a lost a piece of me.

I pulled up my tights and poked his chest as he adjusted his pants. "Okay. That's it, Mister. We can't do this again. It was good sex that we both wanted, and I have no regrets."

Chris smiled and bent to gently give me a smooch as if I didn't say a word. "Come see me tonight."

"I have a date." I folded my arms.

"Really? Is that just an excuse?" He looked down at me with a slight frown.

"No. I really do, and I need to keep it, so I can stop this madness between me and you. I haven't had sex in over a year which is a drought for me. And the moment you touch me I'm ready to jump you. I've had sex with you twice already and don't really know anything about you. We haven't even been on a date."

"I did ask what you were doing later. Let me take you out."

"I didn't say that for you to ask me out. I was explaining why I gave in to you so quickly."

"Or maybe we really were just feeling each other and doing what naturally happens between a man and a woman. I want to get to know you better."

"We can't get to know each other better. I am a new professor with no tenure, if it gets out that I am dating you I can lose my job." I gathered my belongings, knowing that I couldn't be alone in a room with him too much longer. "I can't deny that both times were amazing and we both had fantasies that came to life. But it is what it is. Please, Chris. I really can't do this."

He nodded and put his hands in his pocket. "Got you. It was a fun class. Thank you for indulging me with my fantasy."

I watched him leave out of the class, and though an unexpected pang of sadness washed over me, it was for the best. I picked up my stuff and walked out of the classroom.

Chapter 4: All I need is a distraction

"**I** heard you and Derek are going out tonight? Are you excited?" My cousin, Tamela asked as soon as I answered my cell.

I had just gotten home to my apartment and sat cross-legged on my sofa still thinking of Chris, wondering what would have happened if I spent the day with him. "Yes, I am. I like him and look forward to it. My semester is finally over, and I have a break until after Martin Luther King weekend. I need to go out too. These students be killing me." *And sexing me.* I had to physically shake my head to clear that last thought.

"Well, he can't wait. He really likes you, too."

"Does he know you are telling me these things? I don't want you telling him everything I'm saying to you." That was the one thing I hated about dating someone who your family or friends already know. There was already a level of expectation and pressure that you would work even if it didn't. Derek had been knowing my cousin since college. She had a boyfriend who also knew Derek and they both vouched for him. Tamela left D.C. when she attended Southern University and never returned home after graduation. She had made a life for herself and worked as an insurance representative. I only applied and accepted a teaching position at LSU because she lived in Baton Rouge, though I wasn't planning to remain here forever. I'm more of a big city girl and this was a college town. I was hoping to get tenure or at least move up to Associate Professor before I applied for a new position hopefully back on the East Coast.

"He tells me these things because he wants you to know that he really likes you. I'm so happy. So, what are the plans?"

"You mean he didn't tell you?" I asked sarcastically.

"Of course, but I want to see if the nigga was lying. He is still a man."

"Girl, you are crazy." I laughed. We were only months apart in age and though we grew up in the DC area, we didn't become close until this past year. In D.C., it was just me and my mother. My father had died when I was five and my mother had been over-protective and kept me close and she thought my cousin was too fast. Tamela was the youngest of five and grew up with both of her parents. Her father and my mother were siblings. "We're going to meet up at Tsunami, and we'll see from there."

"He's trying to impress you taking you to that high ass restaurant because he doesn't even like Sushi."

"Oh...he told me he loved Sushi when he asked what I like to eat." We're just getting to know each other. There's no need to lie about something so little. "We definitely could go somewhere else."

"I hear it's nice there. It's probably why he's taking you there. I'm sure he'll find something on the menu."

"I know he's your friend but why lie about that?"

"Well, you are a big-time professor...he probably wants to show you he can be upscale."

"Tam, you do know, you and he both probably make more than I do?"

"Yeah, but when people know that you're Dr. Simone Austin, it can be intimidating for a man."

"I don't introduce myself that way and all I did was remain in school longer and added more student loan debt than you and Derek. I'm no different."

"I know that. I'm just telling you how men might see you. Derek is trying to impress you that's all. Don't make a big deal about this sushi thing. In fact, don't tell him I said anything."

"Okay, I won't." I tapped my pen against my bag, trying hard not to let something so minor bother me.

"Please say you're going for sexy tonight?"

I wasn't initially, but after Chris, I felt the need to do something that may spur Derek to be a little more sexual towards me. He had been so respectful and had avoided any talk of sex. After having a man who was so straight up about what he wanted, I needed Derek to be more upfront. Anything to keep me from wanting Chris. "I am. I'm debating on whether to wear this black dress and black knee-high boots."

"As long as you're showing either cleavage or ass - which you have plenty. If you can show off both even better." It was a running joke in my family that my mother must have drunk plenty of milk because I got all the curves in my family. The women in my family tended to either be rail thin or thick and I was the only one in between.

"My dress does show off both or I could go for jeans, a tight turtleneck and heels. Save my dress for another occasion. I'm sure there'll be another date. It's Christmas time and I love spending time with a man during this time of year. It's been a minute since I did."

"Maybe we can double date and go to New Orleans for dinner and Celebration in the Oaks."

"What's that?"

"It's really romantic and we walk through City Park and look at beautiful Christmas light displays, listen to a jazz band, and drink hot chocolate."

"Sounds cool. Maybe." I smiled feeling like I might just be able to have a social and a work life here. I had been lonely though I didn't like to tell anyone, though Bea had guessed it because she knew me the best.

"No, maybe. Let's plan for it. Sam wants to go next weekend. Just ask Derek while at dinner tonight."

"What if the date is horrible?"

"You already are attracted to each other and you met for coffee. You really think it's going to be horrible?"

I shrugged my shoulders as if she could see me. "I guess not. And you and I are still going to be cool, if Derek and I don't end up together?"

"Monie, you my cousin, first. Of course. But why do you

think it won't work? You called me after you had coffee and said it went well. What happened since then? Did he say something that bothered you?"

"No... I just..." I debated whether to tell her about Chris. Not that I thought my cousin would judge me but telling someone would make him real. Was I ready for it to be real and not just my secret?

"Just what?"

I looked at the ceiling before responding quickly, "I might have met someone else."

"What? Who?" Disbelief and surprise in her voice.

"I probably should not say anything."

"Who is it?"

"One of my students, sort of hit on me and he's really cute. Don't judge me." I wasn't ready to tell her we already had sex the minute we were alone.

"A student? You like them young? Okay...I see you." Tamela giggled.

"No, crazy. I like them my age. He's an older student. Well, he's twenty-six."

"Can you date your students? Isn't that illegal or something?"

"Not illegal but grounds for suspension or dismissal. Although the male professors mess with students all the time and from what I hear nothing happens. I saw one of my male colleagues at the movies on the other side of town with a girl who was in my class. But I know if I was caught, especially being a new professor at a white university, I would be done."

"Typical double standard."

"Yep. I mean technically he's no longer my student after this semester, so I'm not sure how that works. It might be okay after a certain time. Still not a good look to even to be known as someone who sleeps with students."

"How do you know he likes you?"

"He told me."

Tam said in disbelief, "So, he just told you? Just like that?

What did he actually say?"

"He told me he was attracted to me and couldn't stop thinking about me during my office hours." *And that he wanted to fuck me, and he did.* I wanted to add.

"Wow. Students bold now."

"Really bold," I confirmed getting turned on again thinking of Chris and how he had me bent over in my classroom earlier today.

"Is he really cute?"

"Girl, he's so handsome and fine that I had to keep reminding myself during the semester that he was my student. Honestly, I had a little crush on him and didn't know he felt the same until he asked me out. I told him we couldn't, but I don't know..."

"What Bea, say?"

"I haven't told her yet?"

"What the hell? You tell her everything. You won't make a move without her. I used to think you wouldn't take a dump without her knowing."

"Really, Tam?" Tam and Bea could not stand each other. They really were just alike, and both had large personalities. I've tried several times over the years to get them to like each other but it never worked.

"Alright...alright. I feel honored that you told me first. I think you should just go out with Derek who you said is also handsome. That student sounds like nothing but trouble. You can't even date him publicly. You want a relationship and I don't see that being possible with him."

"What if I don't want a relationship?" I tugged on my footie.

Tam snorted. "Since when? You've been wanting to be married forever."

"I know, but maybe I've been going at it all wrong. Maybe I'm not married because I
make that too much of a focus." It's true I have wanted to be married ever since I could remember. What I did know and could remember of my parents, they loved each other deeply.

My mother never remarried because she loved my father so

much. She had been
devastated when he was killed in a car accident on the way home
from work. I remember being sad but sadder for my mother at the
funeral. I loved my father, but I was so young when he died. I remember that he always seemed happy and would kiss and hug me
and my mother all the time. I guess I had always hoped to have
the same relationship that my parents did. My mother had married young, had me, and was a widow by the time she was twenty-
seven and I always thought I would have at least been married by
now.

I sighed, "I might put too much pressure on my relationships."

"That sounds like Bea talking. Ain't nothing wrong with
asking for what you want. You want to be married then you
should date a man who wants that too. And Derek wants to be in
a relationship. If he didn't, I wouldn't be trying to hook you two
up."

"I hope one day you and Bea will get along because you have
her all wrong. Bea just thinks I should date without the whole
pressure of commitment. She wants to be married too. And yes, I
know Derek wants to be in a relationship, it's one of the things I
like about him."

"Well, then be flattered by the attention of your student
and put your energy into Derek."

"Yeah, you're right." I tapped the set of exams next to me. I
glanced down and did a double-take. Chris's exam was on top and
he had written a note. "Oh..."

"What?"

"Nothing, just grading exams. Yeah. You're right. Go ahead
and plan for us to go with you to New Orleans next week. I'll ask
Derek and call you after I get home tonight."

"I'm hoping you won't call me until tomorrow."

"Why are you so crazy? It's too soon," I said though it really
wasn't. I just wasn't into having sex with two different men on the
same day. "I got to go and get some work done before tonight."

"Okay, talk to you later."

"Yeah." I put down my cell and picked up his exam.

I want to see you again. Here's my address. You already have my phone number.

He had written it in pencil. I looked at his address and noticed he lived two exits away on the highway from me. I could be with him in a matter of a few minutes. I pulled my knees in my chest, rocking back and forth. If I wanted to, I could spend the rest of the day in his bed. I shut my eyes tight as if I could close my brain from the memories of us fucking. Ignorance is truly bliss, knowing he was so close to me caused too much turmoil. All I had to do was erase his message and I could focus on Derek. He wanted a relationship and Chris probably only wanted sex.

"And don't forget he may not be your student anymore, but he's still a student," I said to myself as I grabbed a pencil on my coffee table and quickly erased his message before I could change my mind.

∞∞∞

Several hours later, I sat across from Derek at Tsunami, glad that I decided to go out on this date. We had a view of the river and it was a beautiful restaurant. He looked nice tonight with his dark slacks and sweater, much nicer than when I first met him. I was attracted to him the minute I saw him at Thanksgiving when he walked in my cousin's door all smiles. At right under six feet, light skinned with brown eyes and dark brows, he was handsome. His hair was naturally curly, and he wore it shaved on the sides but fuller on top. He used to play college football and remained fit. Derek had a warm smile and genuinely seemed to be a good guy. He'd married when he was nineteen to his high school sweetheart. They both realized they got married too young and divorced two years ago. We were the same age and he had a good job and more importantly he wanted a relationship.

"Okay, when are you going to admit you don't like Sushi?" I asked once we were served our food. He had struggled ordering from the menu and had settled for steak. He could not hide his displeasure when it was served with Bok choy and mashed wasabi. I took a bite of my shrimp tempura.

"You got me. I don't like it." He laughed as he played with his food.

"We're going to have to get something to eat after this." I smiled. "Or at least for you, I'm enjoying my dinner. That will teach you for lying to me."

Derek looked sheepish. "I know. I shouldn't have told you I loved it."

"Yeah, 'love' is pretty strong when you obviously don't like it at all. You don't have to lie about anything to me. We're just getting to know each other. If we fit, we fit. You don't have to put on airs for me."

"I see that I don't. You're one cool lady. It won't happen again." He took a swig of imported beer.

"So, tell me, what do you really like to eat?"

"I'm good with buffalo wings and fries."

"Like Buffalo Wild Wings?" I guessed. He did seem more of a simple guy.

"Yeah."

"Okay, we can go there after this, if you want. I can get a drink or something." I didn't want the night to end, we were having fun and he kept me from thinking of Chris.

"You're sure?"

"Yeah. You need to eat."

"Or we can go back to my place?" He reached for my hand and held it. No sparks but still nice. "I promise we don't have to do anything but watch a movie. I can whip up a mean turkey sandwich."

"A 'mean' turkey sandwich? What if I make you something to eat? We can stop at the store and I can pick up a few things and make you something quick. You like pasta alfredo with chicken?"

I trusted him enough to know I could go to his home and chill if that's all I wanted to do.

"You actually want to cook for me?"

"Yep. I like to cook, just don't since it is only me."

"Well, can we get your food to go? I love pasta and I'm hungry." He joked.

I raised one eyebrow. "Nope. I'm going to enjoy my food and eat some of your steak. I like this restaurant and I want..." I stopped mid-sentence because as I admired the dining area, Chris walked in looking scrumptious in dark slacks and a light polo. He held the hand of a beautiful woman whose dress was a tad too tight for my taste. He and his date headed to the bar and she immediately leaned in to him and whispered something in his ear. I could see his dimple from across the room when he pulled out her chair so she could sit. *What the hell?*

"Everything okay?" Derek asked concern in his voice and he started to turn his head in the direction of my gaze.

I squeezed his hand hoping to keep his attention before I let it go. "Yeah, it's fine. I thought I saw some students. Occupational hazard being a professor in a small city. I don't like going places my students frequent. Unfortunately, like Buffalo Wild Wings." I tried to act unaffected by Chris' arrival. *I can't believe this shit.*

"Oh, then why did you say it was okay to eat there? Honesty goes both ways."

"Touché. Yeah, well I can't avoid every restaurant, so if that's what you like to eat, that's fine with me." I found myself drawn back to the bar and could see them laughing. They looked good together and I wondered if she was his girlfriend. I had to stop staring at him before Derek noticed. I returned my attention my own date. "Can you wait that long for me to cook? You probably really hungry?"

"I can eat more of the steak, it's not bad and should hold me until you finish cooking for me. Do you want to go to New Orleans with Tam and Sam next week?"

I really wanted to go now before Chris saw me. I snuck another peek at him and his date as I pretended to laugh at hearing how my cousin and her boyfriend's names rhymed. "I don't think I ever heard their names said together. That's hilarious, don't you think?"

He looked confused at first and then he smiled. "I thought you were laughing at me for asking you about New Orleans...I guess I never thought of it but yeah, it is kind of funny."

"I wouldn't laugh at you. I was supposed to ask *you* about New Orleans. Figures Tam brought it up to you too. Yeah, let's go. I'm off until after MLK weekend so I have plenty of time to do whatever," I said now even more determined to put a certain sexy man, only a few feet away from me out of my mind. Obviously, he was already involved with someone, so I should enjoy the company of Derek and see where this goes. I took a sip of my wine and peeked over my glass behind Derek and caught Chris staring back at me. Embarrassed at getting caught, I averted my gaze to Derek who was cutting up his steak. My nerves officially fraught now that Chris saw me. I really needed to go right now.

"You're not eating? You sure you don't want to wrap this up and leave?" Derek observed.

I noticed my trembling hands and hid them under the table. I needed to regain my senses and enjoy the rest of my date, which now seemed impossible. "Yes, let's just get this to go. I need to go to the restroom." I stood hurriedly and picked up my purse.

"You okay?" He half-stood.

"Yeah, yeah. I'm fine. I'll be right back." I headed the restroom which thankfully was the opposite direction of the bar. I didn't want to walk past him.

Once in the bathroom, I checked the three stalls, grateful I was alone. I stared in the mirror at myself, holding on to the sink, taking deep breaths trying to calm myself. Chris was on a date and they seemed comfortable with each other, so it wasn't a first date. It just proved that he wants sex and Derek wants more. He only asked you out to have more sex and Derek hasn't approached me about sex yet and we're already planning future dates. But why was Chris so damn sexy? Ugh. I don't want to like him but my body, my body was a different story.

"It doesn't matter that I'm more attracted to Chris, it's not going to end well." I took one more deep breath and smoothed my hair, styled in an inverted bob. I did look sexy myself tonight, glad I wore the dress. As I touched the doorknob, I had to fight the urge to go to Chris so he could make me feel hot with just a glance. I wanted to be sexy for him. I gritted my teeth. I had to get the fuck out of this restaurant.

When I opened the door to the restroom, Chris leaned on the wall next to the door and smiled down at me. "Hey."

Chapter 5: Mad attraction

I almost screamed and clasped my hands in front of me trying to hide my surprise and renewed nervousness at his presence. "Are you stalking me?" I asked annoyed though I was anything but.

"You're the one eye stalking me," he said with a slow smile.

I rolled my eyes mad at myself that he caught me staring at him. "Why are you bothering me anyway? You see I'm with someone."

"Whatever... You haven't been able to stop staring at me since I walked in here." Chris taunted. "You weren't even in there long enough to do anything. The moment you got caught watching me, you suddenly had to use the restroom. Stop playing games, you hoped I followed you back here."

"That's not true. You get on my..." My protest was cut off by his tongue. He pushed me back in the restroom roughly, hands already cupping my ass. I kissed him back hungrily wanting him desperately, already weak for him.

"Wait...wait, Chris," I said between kisses giving up the fight. I was resigned to be his, if only for a moment. "I'm not about to do it in the restroom."

"The way I'm going make you feel you won't care where we are." He promised as he began to kiss my neck. "I didn't think you could get sexier...this dress..."

"Mm..." I couldn't stop the grin that I did get to look sexy for him. My hands were under his light blue sweater rubbing his muscled back, enjoying his attention to my neck when I thought about Derek waiting for me. "Fuck...fuck. This is so wrong. I am on a date and so are you. She looks like your girlfriend."

"Well, he doesn't look like your boyfriend." His soft lips felt good against my neck as his fingers toyed with the edges of my panties.

I stopped his roaming hand. "What should my boyfriend look like?" Noting that he didn't deny his date was his girlfriend.

He gave me a slow, delicious kiss before meeting my eyes. "Like me."

My heart stopped beating at his simple answer and I pressed my hand flat against his chest. "Are you bringing her home tonight?"

His eyes were now half-closed as he looked down at me. "No."

"Why?"

"Because you're spending the night with me." He kissed my forehead, the sweetest move he could have made at that moment. "You have my address."

I didn't bother to deny the truth as I ran my hands down to his abs and I felt his stomach quiver. "I have a date."

"You mean with me?" He asked playfully as he cupped me over my panties.

I smirked and moved against his hand that rubbed me gently, making me so wet with need. "You're funny."

"Make some excuse and come see me later. You're right, I don't want to do it in this restroom." He quickly reached to hold the door close with his free hand when someone tried to open it. I could hear the woman outside complain. "Better say yes, so I can let this woman in here."

"You're so irritating." I tried to move his other hand from my panties, and he cupped me harder.

Chris continued to press against the door with one hand. "Simone..."

"Fine. Give me an hour or so." Once again, I pretended to be bothered but internally doing cartwheels.

While still holding the door firmly, he removed his hand from under my dress, tongued me briefly, before he pulled open the door. He smiled widely at the shocked older woman standing on the other side. "Sorry, we needed some privacy."

She looked flustered but managed to speak. "No problem."

My eyes followed him helplessly as he strode ahead full of swag, and I stopped right outside the restroom to get myself together. The woman noticed me inert. "Young lady, don't be a fool, you better go get that man."

I looked at the woman who had her arms folded like she meant business. "Ma'am you're absolutely right." I could no longer pretend that I didn't want him or that I was just horny. The attraction between us was simply on another level and we were like two magnets drawn to each other.

I stood by the restroom trying to come up with a reason to end the date after promising Derek a home cooked meal. Grateful I grabbed my purse, I pulled out my cell. Bea was on a date, but I needed her.

Help!! 8:37pm

She immediately called. "What's wrong?"

"I am so sorry for bothering you on your date but it's an emergency."

"Girl, I'm back at home. He was boring and a total waste of time. Next." She laughed. "What's the emergency? Aren't you out with Derek?"

"Yes, but Chris showed up, pushed me in the bathroom and kissed on me and now wants me to spend the night with him. I want to so bad, but I don't know how to get out of hanging out with Derek because I promised him, I would cook pasta for him tonight. What do I do?" I whispered loudly in the phone.

The woman, who we locked out of the restroom, came out the door. "You're still here?"

"Yeah, I don't know what to do. I'm already on a date and that man you saw is not my date, but I really, really like him, and he wants me to be with him tonight." I don't know what possessed me to tell this perfect stranger anything. And I could hear Bea trying to figure out if I was speaking to her.

"So, you have to get out of a date?"

"Yes. He is a nice guy too but...   'v

"But the guy I saw is hotter right?"

"I mean both are good looking, I just..."

"You want to be with the other man more." She then asked with a concerned frown, "Are any of these men your boyfriend?"

I shook my head still holding my phone, hearing Bea curse me since I wasn't speaking to her. "No, I don't have a boyfriend."

"I'll help. Let me speak for you. Come on." The woman walked briskly ahead on a mission.

"What? What are you going to do?" I hurried after her until she slowed so I could take the lead.

"Just be quiet once we get to the table."

I could still hear my best friend yelling. "Bea, got to go. Will explain in a few minutes, I promise." I clicked off the phone to her protests.

"What's your name?" My new friend asked.

"It's Simone and what's yours?"

"Your 'Fairy Godmother'."

I laughed and looked back at her. "You're really are. Making my dreams come true, at least for tonight."

As we walked back to the table, I looked towards the bar and Chris sat next to his date, who had a possessive hand on his thigh. When he saw me with the woman from the restroom, I could see his confused expression. I glared at him quickly, hoping he could read my mind that he better be without that woman, at his place as he promised, if I'm ruining a good date. I went back to my table and Derek smiled with relief before frowning when he noticed the woman behind me.

"Is everything okay?"

"I..." The woman nudged me when I started to speak and moved to stand in front of me.

"I'm so very sorry. Simone is my neighbor and I really need her help. She told me she was on a date with you, but I really need her. It's a personal problem. She will make it up to you."

I could see the disappointment on Derek's face, and my stomach panged with guilt. "I'm sorry but..." I saw a movement. Chris and his date stood to leave, and anticipation replaced the guilt. "I really have to go. Maybe we can get together during the week and I will talk to Tam about New Orleans for next week."

"Oh...okay. Do you need my help?" He asked standing up with concern etched on his face.

"No, no baby...it's a private manner." My "godmother" patted his arm sweetly and spoke to me, "Did you drive your own car?"

"I did." Glad I met Derek here more than ever. "I can give you a ride home."

"I need to pay my bill first. Just come by my table when you're finished." She smiled at Derek again. "Please don't be mad at Simone, it's not her fault. I hate that I'm messing up her date. I'll give you some privacy." She nodded at me before walking away.

I moved closer to Derek. "I'm sorry. I went to the restroom and ran into her."

"It's fine. I already paid the bill. There's your, to-go box. I added my steak to your box. I think you'll enjoy it more." He gave me a hug and a kiss on the cheek. "Raincheck on the pasta?"

"Of course." I hugged him tighter and whispered in his ear, "Thank you for understanding. I promise to make it up to you."

"I hope so...later, Simone." He grabbed his jacket, pecked my lips this time, and headed out of the restaurant.

I picked up my food and hurried to where "my fairy godmother" ate with two other women. "Good evening, ladies." I leaned down and kissed her cheek. "Thank you."

She smiled. "Both are handsome, but that fine one in the restroom will steal your heart. I would love to know who you'll end up with."

"Me too." I laughed. "Can I have your real name and number and I will keep you posted?"

I called Bea, the minute I got in my car. I pleaded, "Don't curse me out, okay? I know I sounded crazy but, in a nutshell I'm on my way to have the most amazing sex with one of my students."

"Are you fucking serious right now? Not the fine ass student you been crushing on that you told me you were over?"

"Yes, the one and only."

"Not just a date but on your way to have sex? I thought I was the THOT out of the two of us. Explain."

"His name is Chris and he came to my office hours on Monday and told me he couldn't stop thinking about me and wanted to fuck me -

Girl, he actually said that?" She interrupted.

"Yes, and the next thing I know he had me on my desk. And then today we did it in the class after everyone left when he came to take the make-up final. He asked me out tonight, but I already had a date and then I thought it was best to end things anyway since he is or was my student. So, I went out with Derek, Tam's friend?"

"Already preferring the student. I'll get on your case later, on why I'm just hearing about the sex almost a week later, but I digress."

"I swear you and Tam get on my nerves, I need you both to get along. Anyways Derek is really cool. I told you we had fun when we met up for coffee *and* he wants a relationship."

"With you, already?"

"No, I mean in general. But it could be soon."

"So why are you sexing the student if you're feeling Derek? I mean I know I would, but you and I are different? You're the one ready to be married and birthing babies."

"Because for once, I'm being you. I just want to date and see what happens. Chris is un-fucking believable. Easily the best sex I ever had, and we haven't even made it to a bed yet. He is so damn sexy, and he knows it."

"I'm so confused. So, were you on a date with Derek when you called me?"

"Yep. And Chris came to the same restaurant with his date. I went to the restroom to compose myself because I'm trembling and shit because I didn't expect to see him and when I leave the restroom Chris is standing there and pushes me back inside and tries to have sex with me there. He is so freaking hot that I agreed to get out of my date and spend the night with him. And the conversation you heard was an older woman like she could be my Auntie, who caught us in the restroom. For some crazy reason she helped me with my excuse to get out of my date."

"Take a breath. Chill. I can tell you're driving." She was right. I was talking and driving fast. I needed to focus. "You're now on the way to his house?"

"I have to go home first to get his address and get showered again. What should I wear?"

"A 'fuck me' dress."

"I'm already wearing it." I laughed. "It's the reason I got the chance to leave one good looking man to go sex another one."

"Okay, I got an idea. Fuck him up and come over wearing pajamas. You spending the night, right? Make it like a slumber party and have fun. I'm loving this...so exciting." She squealed before asking, "You think you messed up things with Derek?"

"No, my 'fairy godmother' took care of that. She pretended that she was my neighbor who needed my 'help' and I think he believed her. She was an older woman so of course he believed her. Plus, we're supposed to double date with Tam next Saturday in New Orleans. I'm good on that end."

"Now, isn't this more fun than wondering if either one of them wants a committed relationship? And spending countless hours looking for signs and trying to decipher everything he does or doesn't do?"

"Yeah. It is." It did feel good to have some control over my dating life instead of waiting and hoping someone would call me. I had the potential to date two different men.

"I suggest you keep it that way unless one of them really makes you want more."

"Ultimately, it will have to be Derek because I can't openly date a student."

"Like I said, keep it open until one of them really makes you want more, and he wants the same. Make no decisions until you do. Monie, just have fun, okay?"

"I'm already having fun. Didn't you hear me when I said I've had amazing sex twice this week and haven't even made it to the bedroom yet?"

Chapter 6: *Kicking it*

I drove behind a car into his gated apartment complex, which was more expensive than mine. I'd considered this one when I hunted for housing. He must have a good job and go to school. As I searched, for his building, I realized I didn't know even basic information about him beyond that he was a business major. Maybe it was time to know him beyond his physical and intellectual attributes.

Nervously, I knocked on his door, second-guessing coming over without calling. And then I didn't even have to buzz him to open the gate. What if he changed his mind or he couldn't get rid of his date? He didn't have my number to call me. I could pretend I have the wrong apartment if she's there. My apprehension grew the longer I stood and the moment I was about to run back to my car, he opened the door to his apartment with a smile. "Sorry, I was in the bathroom when I heard the bell."

Chris now wore a black Nike tank with coordinating basketball shorts, his biceps on front street. And then he had the nerve to smell so fresh and so clean.

I bopped my head to the song that now played in my head.

He gave me a curious glance before he took my coat and hung it in his closet by the front door. He grabbed my overnight bag from my hand. "Are you listening to music?"

"Umm...I just had a song in my head." I stood there trying to calm myself. "You smell good and I thought about that Outkast song."

His forehead wrinkled and then he cracked a smile before walking in front of me. "You like rap. I bet you must like to dance?"

"I'm a world class chair dancer." I watched him bring my bag in what I'm guessing is his bedroom and my stomach clenched at the thought of what he would do to me there.

"Not a club person?" He called.

"At all, especially because here in Baton Rouge, I would be partying with my students."

"I'm not into the club scene either and not much of a dancer. You want something to drink?" Chris came back into the main room.

"Not right now." I moved into his spacious living area. He had a dark brown leather sofa with matching love seat on white carpet. CNN played in the background on his large flat screen attached to the wall. This was his home and though we'd had sex, somehow this felt more intimate like we were headed for a relationship. Maybe this wasn't a good idea. I couldn't be Bea and just date. Seeing his space and I was already half in love.

He stood slightly behind me and put his arm around my shoulders. "It's okay. Relax. We have all night."

"Um...when you say things like that it makes me even more nervous." I stepped out of his embrace.

Chris pulled me back into him, wrapped his arms around me from behind, and tucked his head by my neck. "I meant we can do whatever we want. We can watch TV, talk, eat chips, we can just get to know each other... whatever you decide."

His unexpected warmth relaxed me, and I tilted my head to look back at him. "So, you would be okay with no sex?"

"Yeah. And based on this grown ass onesie you're wearing I'm guessing you don't want sex." He tugged on my all in one pajamas footies included.

I playfully unzipped and zipped, exposing the top of my breasts. "Easy access in case we do have sex."

I felt his laughter against my back. "I see. No pressure for real. We can just chill and get to know one another."

"Seriously? What about what happened in the restroom? You were about to jump me there." I was completely myself now.

"And I want to jump you here but I'm good if you just let me hold you." He squeezed me tighter.

I closed my eyes loving his embrace, so safe and warm especially after the bitter cold. We were bordering on relationship territory and I couldn't stop myself from asking. "What do you want from me?"

"Whatever you want to give me," he said in a low, deep voice.

"Not good enough. Do you just want to be fuck buddies or be in a relationship?" Bea would kill me right now, but I still needed to define what we were doing even if it wasn't anything.

"Simone...is it okay to call you that?" He asked. "I mean I wouldn't want to offend your sensibilities by not getting permission to call you by your first name, though I have been inside you twice already."

My lower half tingled at hearing him say my name and at the reminder of him being inside of me. "Yes, Simone is fine. I'm not your teacher anymore"

"Good, because I don't need to hear every time, we have sex between tonight and tomorrow how I'm your student, blah, blah, blah." He kissed my neck.

"Such a big ego. Besides, I thought we didn't have to have sex?"

"We don't. I'm taking your lead and I already know what you want." Chris rocked slowly with me in his arms, still kissing me.

"Really? You're the aggressor in this." I smiled enjoying his lips on my neck.

He lifted his head. "And who opened her legs in her office and then today demanded I fuck her earlier?"

"Demanded? I just gave you permission. You're the one who initiated with a kiss."

"Operative word, a kiss. I didn't expect we would have sex, that first time or today."

I laughed and turned around to face him. "You masturbated using my hand and you didn't think it would end in sex?"

He raised one eyebrow. "No. I would have stopped at the four play."

"You lie, Mr. Alexander." I poked his chest.

"Okay, let's make a bet. Whoever initiates sex between tonight and whenever you leave is the loser."

"Whenever I leave?" I questioned though I was pleased. *He really likes me and wants my company.*

"Focus, Simone," he chastised. "If you win, I'll clean your office and your car. My guess is your house is a mess too judging by your office and car. So, I will clean that as well."

"Hey, you and your classmates said you weren't going to judge my car when I showed pics of my car to the class." I looked at the neatness and order in his apartment while mine looked like a tornado hit at any given time. "Okay, I see you're a neat freak. I wish I could lie but my life is a mess. My car alone is a job. I'll take that bet but you don't have to do my office. Just my house and car. Now, what do I have to do if you win, which I highly doubt?"

He rubbed his hands together like he was masterminding something evil and began walking around me.

"Maybe I should come up with my own terms. You're scaring me," I said half-serious. I stood there feeling like a two-piece spicy at Popeyes as he assessed me from every angle. "Come on, tell me."

Chris stopped once he got back in front of me and with folded arms, said, "You will go away with me for Valentine's Day."

Shit. My hands trembled and again I clasped them together in front of me, so he couldn't see how he affected me. "That's two months away...and it's Valentine's."

"I know that. Deal?" He didn't sound as certain as he had been, and I looked at his defensive stance. "If you don't want to go just make sure you win the bet."

Without answering, I went to his brown leather sofa and sat down. "Valentine's Day? What exactly do you want from me? I noticed you avoided the question."

He moved to sit next to me. "I meant what I said, whatever you want to give me. I respect your position as a professor. So, if you just want to fuck, we can. And if you want to date, we can. But I'm not good in relationships."

"So why ask me out for Valentines' Day before Christmas? That's the surest sign for a woman that a man wants commitment and you're making it hard for me to keep it at a sexual level."

"It's just a trip. I only thought about a trip mainly because I want to be out in the open without you worrying about getting caught. And I feel like you plan to disappear on me after tomorrow, so I wanted to be sure I see you again."

If I spent Valentine's Day with Chris anywhere on this Earth, I would be so in love and something told me that he or I weren't ready for that type of emotion yet. I took a deep breath. "Okay, I'll agree to the bet. But I want us to be honest with each other while we don't care enough to hide the truth."

Chris looked at me. "Okay, what do you want to ask me?"

"Was that your girlfriend earlier?"

He answered, "No, we've been kicking it."

"If I didn't say 'yes' tonight, would she be here?"

At my annoyed expression, he argued, "Yes, just like I'm sure you would have been with that dude."

"I wasn't going to have sex with him tonight, like I'm sure you would have."

He shrugged. "Why weren't you going to have sex with him?"

"I don't have sex with two different men on the same day."

"Really? You should try it." He smiled devilishly.

"In that case, let me call Derek now, I'm sure he would love to hear from me." I tried to stand, and Chris pulled me back down next to him.

"Joking. Can't you take a joke?" He gave me a dimpled smile. "Who is he, anyway? He let you go too easy tonight for him to be a boyfriend. What was up with that lady in the restroom anyway? Did you know her?"

"Let's just say she's rooting for us and decided to help. I guess your smile got to her."

Chris quickly covered his smile with his hand playfully and spoke through his hand. "Who is the guy?"

"His name is Derek, and this was our second date. I like him.

He's my cousin's friend, and he wants a relationship," I added to see his reaction.

He rubbed the back of my head where my hair tapered into a V. "You plan to keep seeing him?"

"If he forgives me for changing our plans so I could be here."

Chris quietly played in my hair.

After a few seconds passed of silence passed, I asked, "Does that bother you?"

His jaw tightened. "It shouldn't. But it does. Did it bother you to see me with Kat?"

"'Cat'? Her name is 'Cat', like a kitty cat? Are you freaking kidding me?"

"Kat with a 'K'." He ran one finger down my neck causing me to shiver and he smirked. "I got my answer."

I shrugged. "I just think you can do better."

"You don't know her."

"I saw how she was all over you like she's trying to claim you for the world to see with that too tight dress. Like can she breathe?" I commented finding it easy to talk to him like we'd known each other forever. It was like we were already friends. "Does she know that you and she are just 'kicking it'?

"I have never said we were exclusive."

"Oh my God, she definitely thinks she's your girlfriend. That's the oldest trick in the book. You make her feel like it's just you and her. And if she ever catches you with someone else, you can tell her you never said we were committed."

He shook his head. "She knows we just dating."

"Was she pissed when you brought her home? It's Saturday, you're supposed to be with your girlfriend. What did you say to get rid of her?"

"I picked a fight with her." Chris looked guilty.

"Yep, you're her boyfriend. You don't have to lie." I wrapped my arms around his neck. "I hope she's not stalking you and I find my car scratched or tires flattened because she thinks I'm stealing her boyfriend."

He grinned as he placed my legs across his lap. "I'm not her boyfriend."

"Call...I mean text her right now."

"And say what?"

"Apologize for the fight and tell her you're tired but will call her tomorrow. If she responds she wants to come over or ask you to come see her, then you're her boyfriend. Otherwise she's cool with waiting to hear from you."

He pulled out of his phone and texted her. Within seconds she responded.

Chris read it to me. "She was wrong too and wants me to come over...that doesn't prove anything."

"Tell her not tonight but you'll see her soon. I guarantee she'll curse you out."

He did and his phone vibrated soon after. "She said that I was a fucking liar and that I was probably fucking someone else and how could I do that to her after all this time. She ended it with don't fucking call her ever again."

"Mr. Alexander, you don't have to lie." I tapped his nose, though I knew he wasn't, or he wouldn't be so open about her responses.

"I never said we were a couple." His phone shook again. "She's now wondering why I'm not responding. If I cared I would have by now...and yep she told me to fuck myself again."

"Go ahead and respond. I told you I'm not trying to steal her boyfriend."

He raised one brow. "You made your point."

"Let's just kick it too. It's Christmas break. I want to have fun. I really like you and I don't want to mess this up by thinking we could be more. I have a habit of wanting a relationship too soon and run men off because I want a husband and a family. Maybe it's time I learned how to date."

"Why are you being so upfront with me? Not that I'm complaining. I am so for just kicking it." He kissed my lips.

"I want to be different this time around and I'm not a good liar. It was hard to lie to Derek tonight and if 'my fairy godmother' didn't help, I would be cooking him dinner right now instead of here with you."

"You were going to cook for him and all I get is a onesie? I'm thinking that you already like him more."

I slowly unzipped the top of my onesie revealing my naked ample breasts. "You really think I like him more?"

Chris bit his lower lip. "Shit, I'm about to lose this fucking bet."

As he buried his head between my breasts, I rubbed his head, liking my decision to just enjoy the moment without expectations. "Mm... oh, my car and my apartment hasn't been cleaned in over a year. My apartment is the worst."

Chapter 7: Go with the flow

On Monday morning, I made cheese eggs, bacon, and seasoned potatoes, trying to stop the grin that had been constant since Saturday night. We did have sex on the sofa, among other places, and we got into a dispute on who actually lost the bet. At first, he admitted he did until he saw my car. He then said technically, I initiated sex since I flashed him. I argued then if that was his definition, he had been touching or holding me since I walked through the door, so he still lost the bet. In the end, we agreed that he lost the bet and that if we were still "kicking it" by Valentine's Day we would take a trip together.

I was impressed about what I'd learned about him while I'd lain in his arms as we talked all night. He was the oldest of three on his mother's side and the youngest of three on his father's side. His father was several years older than his mother and she had been his second wife. His parents divorced when he was seven years old and she'd remarried and had two daughters. And although they all still lived in Lincoln, Nebraska and he rarely went home, he considered himself very close to his family. I teased saying I had no idea that black people lived in Nebraska. He retorted that there are black folks everywhere, but he didn't want to make a life there and wanted to travel. He joined the Air Force once he graduated from high school, served six years, and currently in the Reserves.

Chris originally came to Louisiana to work on the oil rigs, where he piloted helicopters to transport employees from land to the rigs deep in the Gulf of Mexico. He then decided that he would rather finish his business degree and enrolled in college. Working contract allowed him to be able to handle his bills while he focused on school. Chris planned to graduate next fall and then go right into an MBA program. After he completed his graduate degree, he wanted to own a private charter company. I admitted to him that I was petrified to fly and that I usually drove sixteen plus hours home instead of flying. He promised that he could help me get over my fear of flying. I'd told him it was doubtful, but I appreciated that he even wanted to help me.

"Something smells good." He slung his arm around my neck, breaking my thoughts and pecked my cheek.

"Breakfast is almost ready." I could get used to this intimacy. It's why I wanted to be married. To have a partner to greet and end each day. Since neither of us had to work today, he came over to my place yesterday and spent the night. "You drink coffee? I can make you a cup. I had mine already."

"Not really. Water or juice is fine. You have milk?" He opened my refrigerator, wearing only shorts.

"Almond milk?" I pointed to the carton that was on the top shelf.

His nose scrunched. "Nope. Real milk for me." He picked up apple juice.

"Have you ever tried it?"

"No, but I have had soy and other milk substitutes, give me my whole milk."

"Okay, okay, note for future. He only drinks whole milk. I hope you like eggs, bacon, and potatoes."

"I'm not picky about my food. I'll eat anything. You killed that baked chicken last night. I don't think I ever cared if a woman knew how to cook because my stepdad did all the cooking. But I've officially been spoiled and now anyone who wants to be with me has to cook."

I ladled food on our plates smiling at his praise. "No, no don't do that. Don't make it hard for the next woman. It was just me and my mama, so I learned to cook out of necessity."

"That must have been hard growing up without him." He brought the juice to the counter next to me and poured himself a glass. "You want some?"

"Yes, thank you. It was hard at times but more because my

mother missed him. She really loved my dad and I want the same thing she found in him. I think that's why I get caught up too soon." I looked at him, realizing that I could see such husband potential with him. "A moment of honesty because that's what we're doing, right?"

"Yeah."

"The last two days have been fun, all this togetherness. But we can't keep this up if we're just going to be 'kicking it', I could so fall for you."

He looked down at me and bit his bottom lip, a habit I originally thought was sexual, but he did it too often. "And what would be wrong with that? Oh...the student thing again?"

"No... well, not completely. We still need to be careful in public until enough time has passed. You told me you're not good in relationships. I can fall hard, and I don't want to repeat my patterns of the past."

"Pattern?"

"I fall for men who really don't want the ultimate commitment and it's my fault more than theirs. My last boyfriend told me he wasn't ready for marriage. I just knew sooner or later he would change his mind because we loved one another, and we ended up breaking up because of it. I'm this hopeless romantic believing love prevails no matter what he may say or feel about marriage. With you and even Derek, I want to be different. Just let things flow."

Chris nodded, passed me a glass of juice, and he took a sip of his own before responding, "Is this your way of saying it's time to go? Are you kicking me out?"

I wrapped my arms around his taut waist and rested my head against his muscled chest. "That would be a loud, 'no'. I really, really like you and this has been the best time I've had since I moved here. I just don't want it to be a pattern where we spend all this time together, especially because we live five minutes apart. Look how one night, ended up being two?"

"We're being honest right? I'm not good in relationships, but I already feel like I could be with you." He put down his glass on the counter to hug me back.

I closed my eyes, steeling myself against his words, and opened them to see him staring down at me. "Please, can we just flow? I'm so serious when I say, I can jump all in and scare you off. No, you can't say things like that. I must be with a man who already knows he wants a commitment. We've just been caught up in the moment."

"What if we flow into each other?" He asked his voice deepening.

I backed out his embrace and picked up one of the plates and gave it to him. "Nope, nope, not about to fall for you too early. Boy, you would have me so strung out like a heroin addict. You already got sex out of me way too soon."

Chris grinned as he took his plate and sat at the bar. "Why do you forget to say, you encouraged me to fuck you? Baby, it's been mutual since that first day in class."

"Is that when you started crushing on me?" I sat next to him. "I was wondering if it was then or sometime later."

"The attraction was there the minute I walked in your class. I had to have you." Chris winked at me.

"Oh." He stole my thought for a moment. I glanced at my plate to refocus before asking, "Why did you wait until the end of the semester to say something?"

"Honesty, right?"

"Yep." I took a bite of bacon.

He nudged his shoulder to mine. "It took me that long to work up the courage to say something to you."

I almost choked on my bacon and started coughing. He had to hit my back. Hard. "Okay...okay...I'm...okay...geez...you hit hard...I'm choking on the obvious lie."

"I'm not lying. You were my teacher, remember?"

"Really?" I rolled my eyes. "There was nothing about you that day in my office that was nervous. Who tells their professor he wants to 'fuck' her?"

Chris picked up one of my hands and kissed the back of it. "I tried to stay after class almost every time, hoping you would give me some sign it was okay to step to you. The semester was ending, and I'd become afraid I wouldn't get a chance to tell you how I felt, so I made myself go to your office. I *was* nervous until I sat in front of you and saw how much you wanted me too. At that point I was like fuck it and told you what I wanted. I meant it when I said I can't stop thinking about you. Like the way I feel right at this very moment with you sitting next to me is that I never want this to end."

I tried to pull my hand away and he held on and entwined our fingers. "Simone, if we're going with the flow, then don't stop anything that happens between us. If you want to see me, come see me. If I want to see you, I will. So, what if you fall hard for me? Maybe I'll fall right back." Chris gazed into my eyes and kissed me slowly with his tongue making me hot. He pulled back the moment I returned his kiss and he grabbed a piece of toast. "I think we need to finish eating because I need the energy to clean your car and apartment. Plus, you need to grade exams."

"Wait...you just interrupted... the flow," I said crossing my arms. "I see...making a point?"

"See how aggravating that is, to stop something that feels so good." He chomped on his toast with a smirk. "Eat because you need the energy to ride me as soon as we finish breakfast."

"We both have things to do, remember?"

"Yes, we do and you're one of them." Chris reached between my legs quickly and rubbed my clit before I could close my legs.

I moaned and grinded against his finger before he removed his finger and put it my mouth for me to suck my own juices. "Now, finish eating so we can fuck."

I rolled my eyes, so hot for him, and slowly picked up my fork taking a bite of my eggs, wondering if I could just go with the flow and not rush anything. We were honest with each other thus far and if my feelings start going deep, I'm pretty sure I could tell him so we could either fall back from each other or continue to kick it.

∞∞∞∞

Chris finally left at the crack of dawn on Tuesday in time for him to run home and get ready for work. I walked him to the door and kissed him, refusing to ask him to call me or make plans to see me again. He gave me a hug and popped me on my ass hard, promising to call me later. I simply nodded and once I closed the door, collapsed on the sofa, exhausted after all that sex and all that sexual energy between us when we weren't. I had so many missed calls, including Derek. I would call him back first. I had to do something to make me shake Chris, who I already missed.

I grew moist thinking about the past few days. We were both insatiable. Either he or I would initiate sex the minute the mood hit. At one point I had been grading exams while he vacuumed in front of me, listening to his headphones, still only wearing long shorts. I didn't realize how many muscles were used when one vacuums. He just seemed seem so virile, which he had proven over and over already. I wore only his shirt and I opened my legs where I sat on the sofa. I took the cord that trailed behind him and placed it against my clit. When he would move the vacuum, the cord ran up and down my pussy, making me shiver in pleasure. Chris was so focused on his task that it took a moment for him to figure out why he'd had trouble with the cord. Once he looked back and saw what I'd been doing with the cord, he couldn't tear his eyes away from my pussy and in a matter of seconds he had turned off the vacuum and ate me out with my legs around his head.

I heard my cell ring, waking me up. I must have dozed off thinking of Chris. My cell was in my bedroom. Still tired, I stumbled to my room to get it. I finally got to my phone in time to answer it. "Yeah."

"Simone?"

I sank on the bed, hearing Derek's voice. "Yeah, it's me."

"I wanted to check on you since you had to leave on Saturday, and I hadn't heard from you. You okay? You don't sound like yourself."

"Yeah...everything is fine. I've been tired and sleeping a lot since the semester is finally over. I was going to call you today."

"Oh, okay. Well good then I wanted us to have dinner or something tonight?"

My first thought was to make an excuse because I wanted to be free in case Chris wanted to hang out. But that was the "old" me, waiting by the phone for a man to call. "I would like that. You want to do Buffalo Wild Wings?"

"Or we can go somewhere else nicer," he offered.

"Nope, wings sound good. I did feel bad that I couldn't cook for you. I promise I will soon. My place is too much of a mess to invite you over tonight." My apartment had been a mess until Chris cleaned it and now it looked brand new. In reality, it was too soon for another man to be here when I could still smell another man's scent. I was still me. Just a new and improved one or so I hoped.

"You could always come over to my place." At my hesitation he quickly continued, "Don't worry about that, we have plenty of time to cook for each other. Is six, okay?"

I looked at my cell and noticed it was after one in the afternoon and I still had a lot of grading to do. I'd been asleep for hours. "Make it seven."

"Okay."

I got off the phone and began to peruse my missed calls and texts since I had been ignoring my cell since Saturday night. Chris's phone stayed on the kitchen table as if he didn't want to be disturbed while we were together, either.

I called Tam first. "Hey, girl. Sorry I've been busy."

"I know you were busy. I was worried about your ass and did a drive by and saw your car Sunday night and lights on. Who were you entertaining because it wasn't Derek?"

"The student." I figured why lie.

"Why? I thought you liked Derek?" Her voice slightly raised.

"I do. Just keeping all options open."

"Is that why you left him hanging Saturday night to be with another man?"

"He called you?"

"No, I called him to see how everything went, when you didn't answer your phone. He said you had to leave to check on your neighbor. What neighbor?"

"Tam, a long story but please stay out of it. We're both grown and who's to say he's not seeing anyone else? He's not my boyfriend."

She huffed. "That still doesn't excuse you leaving him at the restaurant."

"Technically, he left me, and we'd been together for two hours so the date could have been almost over. Besides I'm having dinner with him tonight and we still on for Saturday, right?"

"Yes," she said grudgingly.

"Look, I know you don't want him to be mad with you if we don't work but it's a risk when you're dating. I can't be monitored and questioned about everything we may or may not do. Pretend he's not a friend and that I'm your cousin telling you about the guy she's dating. He's good people. I just want to see someone else at the same time until I figure if I should be committed. I'm trying to date this time and not get so caught up."

"You already caught up. That student got you sprung. You left another man to be with him."

"Let's not forget, you were out there bad for a while, having fun, Tam and then you came in once you met Sam. I'm not sprung, he's just fun. Let me enjoy."

"Alright, alright...wait, why are you just calling me? Has he been with you all this time?"

"He left this morning."

I heard her sigh. "Derek doesn't have a chance. I know you and if that dude has been with you this long, he's probably feeling you too."

"I don't know about all that. We are both just having fun and he didn't have to work until today. And Derek does have a chance because this thing with the student is just about sex. I can't realistically date him anytime soon, anyway. I'm just having fun, I promise."

"Is it that good?"

"We have crazy chemistry." I laid back in the bed we had been sexing in since Sunday night, making me miss him all over again. "It's why I'm having dinner with Derek. I got to clear my head before I get too fucked up with him. I can't let lust rule my common sense."

"Lust have ruled my life way too many times. As long as you don't confuse love with lust like I did," Tam admitted.

"Should I be honest with Derek?"

"That you fucking another man? I know it's been awhile since you had a man, but I don't care if he doesn't have a right to be mad, he'll be pissed. You tell him you were with another man who you plan to keep seeing, then you have effectively ended any possibilities with him."

"Chris, wasn't mad when I told him about Derek?"

"Is that his name?"

"Yes."

"Well, of course, Chris is cool with it. He just wants sex. Derek wants more. Don't tell Derek anything because you owe him nothing. Just don't fuck over him, okay? He's one of the good ones."

"I know, I know. I won't. I plan to date him and give him a chance. If it gets serious, I will leave Chris alone. I don't cheat in relationships."

"Alright, have fun tonight and I don't care if Chris wants to see you tonight, tell him you can't."

"He probably won't since we spent the last two days here at my place."

"Do you hear yourself? You sound like you can't say 'no' to him. It doesn't matter if he calls or not, you have a date."

"I'm just saying that I doubt he will call."

"And I'm saying, get your shit together before you're running behind a man who just wants one thing. I had fun and knew when to let go even if it hurt, at least most of the time. You are not me or Bea. Watch yourself."

"I will. Tonight, will be fun and Saturday night in New Orleans is going to be even more fun."

"Can't wait. I love Christmas lights. I'll text you before the end of the week, with all the deets."

"Alright." A text came in as I clicked off the phone.

Can't get you out of my head. Meet me at my place. I'll be home by six. 2:05 pm

My heart beat hard in my chest. I really thought he wouldn't contact me for a few days. The urge to see him was so strong. I sat there with my cell in my hand at a crossroads of sorts. I had to figure this out for myself and not call Bea. I texted him back.

Can't stop thinking about you either, but I can't tonight. Tomorrow? 2:11 pm

He didn't text back and as I got ready for my date, I wondered if I made the right decision to go ahead with Derek.

Chapter 8: Distraction not working

"**W**e have a winner." I laughed as I watched Derek devour his chicken wings. "You definitely prefer this to sushi."

"You not too upset about that are you?" He asked as he wiped his mouth. "You kind of disappeared after that night and I didn't know if I messed up with you."

"Naw...really just needed a break. The semester is rough and I'm still grading papers. I turned my phone off so I could focus. And when you called, I had already decided to call you. You just beat me to it."

"So, what are your favorites?"

"What do you mean?" I took a swig of beer.

"It's still funny to me that you drink beer. Most women don't like beer."

"I started drinking it in graduate school because it was all I could afford." I shrugged my shoulders and looked around the restaurant, hoping I didn't have a repeat of Saturday night. Students were everywhere and the last thing I needed to see was Chris especially with that Kat woman.

"Got ya. I wanted to know your favorites. You know like favorite color? Singer?"

"Oh... I'm girlie and love the color pink. And still love Chris Brown, tatts and all." I found myself unable to completely focus on Derek because I was nervous that my own Chris would walk in here. *How did people date more than one person at a time?* I'm a nervous wreck.

"We're going to have to find a different restaurant next

time, I can tell you're uncomfortable here."

"What?" I asked as if I didn't understand what he meant, stirring my celery in the buffalo sauce.

"You keep looking around and I see nothing but students around me. I get it you want to leave your work at home. We can chill somewhere else. Let's get the check and I know this cigar bar, you might like since you like beer."

"Yeah." I sighed sadly. I wanted to go home because I couldn't stop thinking of Chris and wasn't being fair to Derek. "Hey, can we just wait until Saturday to stay out late? I really do have a lot of grading to do and it's due by Thursday morning. I probably should have waited to go out until I finished everything, but I wanted to make it up to you."

"It's fine. I'm just glad that you agreed to come out on such short notice." His corners of his mouth turned down, which didn't help my guilt.

"I'm really sorry I haven't been good company but don't forget on Saturday, you're supposed to pick me up first and then we're going to pick up my cousin and Sam. I promise to do better because my work will be done until next semester and I can really enjoy."

After a quick peck on the lips and a reminder to text him once I was home, I got in my car. Once again on my date with Derek, we had good conversation, but I found myself drifting to thoughts of Chris and wondered if our "kicking it" days were already over. I know I shouldn't care but I did, and I hated it. I purposely left my phone in my car to avoid checking my cell for a text from him. I hated that I needed to end a date early with Derek, a perfect gentleman, just because I couldn't get Chris out of my stupid head. Derek had to be and would be my only focus on Saturday night as I walked through my front door. Note to self, I wasn't dating, if I only wanted to see one man.

I'd just tossed my coat on my sofa and walked away, when I heard a notification. I hurriedly reached to pick up my coat and struggled trying to find my phone that in my pocket. I finally found it and opened the text without bothering to see who sent it.

Come over once you done with that other dude. 9:36 pm

Despite the lecture I just gave myself, I jumped up and down like a little girl, excited that he wasn't done with us, and texted back wanting to toy with him.

I told you I don't sleep with two men on the same day. 9:38 pm

If you're answering my text, the only man you want fucking you is me. You better be in my bed before it gets too late. I'm tired. 9:39 pm

I grabbed my coat, not even bothering to put it on as I rushed out the door, ignoring the little voice screaming that I had it bad. "I'm just going with the flow."

∞∞∞

I laid across Chris's lap in leggings and a sweatshirt, reading one of my professional journals, while he sat with his feet propped on my coffee table, wearing only sweatpants watching CNN. It was Friday and we'd eaten breakfast and were now relaxing together. In fact, we had spent every day together since I went to his place on Tuesday night. Even when he went to work on Thursday, he came to my place right after work. He initiated spending time together, in my defense, so I still went with the flow.

"You know what's missing in your apartment?" His deep voice rumbled still gruff because we really hadn't spoken much this morning.

"Is that a ding on my lack of organizational skills?"

"No, though Dr. Austin, that's something you need to work on for the new year." I adjusted myself to sit up next to him, slightly annoyed that organization seemed so easy for him while it was a constant struggle for me. "You need Christmas decorations."

"It's just me and I hardly ever think of decorations unless I'm home."

"This is your home at least for a few years. Make a new tradition and decorate. We can drive to Hammond, so no one knows us and get stuff for my place and yours."

"You want to decorate your place, too? Aren't you going home for Christmas?" My mother was coming here two days before Christmas after I told her I wasn't up to the long drive this year.

"Let's get into the Christmas spirit and it's still early enough in the month. I don't leave until Christmas eve morning so I can still enjoy my decorations. We can shop and grab lunch or dinner there." He stood up, pulling me with him. "Come on. Get ready."

∞∞∞

We spent the day in Hammond, shopping for two Christmas trees and decorations for each tree. I went for a purple and gold tree and he went traditional red and green. Although I felt that we could be open about being together in public, I was touched that he was still careful with me. Instead of holding my hand, he hooked his pinkie finger to mine while we were in Wal-Mart and we didn't let go unless it was to pick up something. I hadn't been shopping with anyone in a long time especially a man who actually wanted to go. We had fun arguing about everything from Marvel vs DC to which store was better, Target or Wal-Mart. I argued since we were shopping in a Wal-Mart, it was the obvious choice. He claimed that Target was better because though pricier their merchandise was of better quality. He only drove to Wal-Mart today because he wanted McDonald's fries while we shopped.

After we bought our decorations, we ate at this local casual style seafood restaurant and shared a platter. We both had margaritas and fought over the last piece of French bread served complimentary with our meal, since we both loved bread. Chris was such a cool person in and out the bedroom it was hard to not want more from him. We had only been seeing each other almost two weeks, counting the first time we had sex, but it felt like I've known him for much longer and I told him that.

"It's because technically I have been seeing and talking to you every week since the end of August."

"You know what I mean."

"I do. But it's why for me the only difference is you're getting to know me. I felt like I got to know you while in class. You're one of the most personable professors on campus. It's why you're already one of the popular ones. Chemistry is hard to make interesting and you could relate it to everyday life. You shared personal stories and it made me want to get to know you outside of how hot you looked in those damn dresses."

I blushed at his compliment glad that I made the extra effort to dress for him. "I have a secret."

"Please tell." He looked around as if others were paying attention and leaned closer.

"I used to dress for you but when I realized what I'd been doing I stopped."

Chris sat back with a pleased smile. "That explains why you went from sexy teacher to cute teacher. I'm impressed. You did that for me?"

"Yeah."

He assessed me for a moment before he responded, "You really like me, don't you?"

"You sound surprised? After what we've been doing these past few days, you're surprised I like you?"

"Hey, I know I'm good in bed but that means you were really liking me before the sex."

"Such modesty."

He shrugged his shoulders nonchalantly. "Just speaking truth."

"Of course, I liked you or we wouldn't have had sex that

fast." I took a sip of my margarita refusing to agree about his sexual prowess though I did. "Do you want to get married one day?" I think the alcohol affected me because the question slipped out of my mouth before the thought really entered my head.

Chris's expression grew somber for a second. "Maybe one day. I have so much I want to do and having a wife means I must consider what she wants when I make decisions. I'm too selfish to do that right now. I'm in Baton Rouge today, but once I graduate, I might be in another city or even another country. I can't just do that to a wife. My father is on his fourth wife and said he would still do it again and my mother and stepfather seem happy, so I guess one day. And before you ask, I wouldn't mind being a father. Preferably after marriage but would be happy even if a baby came first."

He seemed uncomfortable and I touched his hand. "We don't have to talk about anything you don't want to talk about."

"It's cool..." Chris turned his hand so he could hold mine and studied our entwined hands. "You want more, and I know sharing how I feel is a mark against me."

"We just kicking it right?" I smiled trying to change the cloud that now floated over us.

Our eyes met.

"Yeah," he simply said and signaled the waitress for check.

Chapter 9: Caught up

C hris quietly drove us back to Baton Rouge. He didn't seem angry or irritable, just in his own world. I hadn't told him I was going to New Orleans tomorrow and as the night drew nearer, I became nervous. I didn't expect or plan that we would spend every day together and I didn't know if he wanted to spend time this weekend. Once we made it back to his place after first dropping off my decorations at my house, I decided to bring it up. It was now Friday night and we were more than likely going to spend the night together since he insisted, we ride back to his apartment in his car. His rather somber mood had lifted, and we listened to Christmas music, ate popcorn, and drank hot chocolate as we decorated his tree.

"I thought we could decorate mine and then go do yours, but I'm getting tired. We can just do your tree tomorrow," he commented as he placed a red bulb on the tree.

"Chris...I...um..." I held an ornament in my hand waiting to give it to him.

He stopped to look at me with a half-smile. "Sounds serious. What's up?"

"I'm going to New Orleans tomorrow with Derek and my cousin and her boyfriend on a double date. I agreed before -

Okay," Chris responded tersely, cutting me off, and went back to decorating the tree.

"Is that cool?" I found myself asking, though I hated that I did since I didn't need his permission to date.

"Do what you want. We just kicking it, right?" His focus solely on the tree now.

I asked slightly exasperated, "Then why do you seem

bothered?"

He placed another ornament on the tree before he stalked toward his bedroom.

I went after him. "Don't be mad, okay? We've been having fun and we still have to decorate my tree."

"I'm going to the bathroom, stop following me," Chris said annoyed, the minute I stepped foot in his bedroom.

"Fine," I retorted now getting angry too. *How could he be mad when we agreed that this is what we were doing?* I leaned against his bedroom door, waiting to talk to him, until I replayed what I just said to him. I hit my own forehead realizing how much I royally fucked up. I shouldn't have told him about Derek. I could have just lied and said I was spending time with friends, anything but the truth. I thought back to what Tam said that I shouldn't tell Derek about Chris because it would end any chance. Maybe I just ruined my chances with Chris because I assumed it wouldn't matter if I went out with someone else. Did that mean he wanted more? And more importantly, what did I want from him, if he did?

I went back to the living area and resumed decorating the tree, hoping we could really talk. I then heard a knock on his front door. My first instinct was to go to the door and then I thought it wasn't my place to answer his door, so I went to his room. "Chris, someone is at your door."

"Who?" He sounded surprised.

"I don't know. I didn't answer the door."

"I'm coming out in a sec."

Although he didn't tell me, I stayed in his bedroom and closed the door behind him once he reappeared. I went to the door to listen and I didn't hear anything at first and then I heard yelling.

"I know you have another woman in here. Her purse is right there."

Chris said firmly, "You have to go now."

"Not until I see who you're hiding."

"Kat, this is stupid. You showed up uninvited and I'm sorry if you're hurt but this why you call before coming over here."

"You weren't returning my calls. What was I supposed to do?"

"Wait until I call you back or date another man. I really don't care."

She screamed, "So, you just fuck me whenever you want, and it doesn't matter how I feel? Who's the woman you're hiding?" I jumped when I heard a crash.

"Kat, get out now." I could hear that he was trying to control his anger.

Suddenly I heard footsteps charging toward the bedroom door and I backed up unconsciously. I wasn't scared but I didn't want to fight a woman over a man who didn't belong to either one of us. He must have grabbed her before she got to the door because I could hear her yelling loudly, "I know you in there, hiding, scared I'm a beat your ass. He's just using you like he did me. He acts like he into you just to fuck you and then he drops you like nothing! You might think you got something, but he's just a piece of shit!"

Chris growled, "Shut up now. I don't owe you shit. I never pretended we were together. We hung out and we had sex. That's it. Now, get the fuck out of my house. If you come back over here, I'm calling the police."

I went to the door again and listened to more yelling and cursing until I heard the door slam. I slowly opened the door and he was hunched over on the sofa. Kat had turned over his table and Christmas ornaments were everywhere. I started cleaning the mess by the tree, thinking about what she said about him and wondered if I was simply replacing Kat until the next woman who caught his eye.

"Leave it," Chris practically yelled.

I took a breath to keep my voice level. "I can get it."

"I said leave the shit alone." He glared at me. "I can clean up my own mess."

I dropped the ornaments I had in my hand. "Just trying to help. I'm sorry."

"What are you apologizing for?" His tone still irritable.

"She was pissed because of me and if I wasn't then it

wouldn't have gotten ugly." I stood in front of him.

"She shouldn't have brought her ass over here without per-mission. We don't and never had that type of relationship." He looked up at me with a scowl. "You really don't care that Kat came by?"

I waved my hand dismissively. "Huh? What should I have done? Come out of the room and get into a fight over you? That's stupid."

Chris shook his head. "You know what? You can leave too."

"Why? Because I didn't want to get into a fight with a crazy woman when you don't belong to either one of us?"

He snapped his finger. "That's right. I just asked a woman who I've been seeing for a while to leave for you, and you about to go on a date with someone else tomorrow. I'll just call her back because at least she wants only me. Have a nice life." He picked up his cell off the sofa and before I realized it, I knocked it out of his hand.

"I know you're not about to call *that* woman back because you can't get what you want with me?" I pointed my finger in his face. "You want me to leave so you can get her back, I'll go, but don't ever disrespect me like that."

"And what is that I want?" He looked up at me still frown-ing.

"You want me to cancel my plans and I can't do that. I prom-ised him that we would go out."

He averted his eyes. "You think I care what you promised to another man?"

"I'm trying to be honest here. If I cancel on him to be with you than all I'm doing is what I have always done, chasing after someone who doesn't want what I want. You just told me you don't want marriage anytime soon. I can respect that and your reasons why. But I can't get caught up in you knowing that. If we're going with the flow, let's do that. And if it gets too hard for either of us, we'll just stop seeing each other."

"Just stop seeing each other? Maybe I can't do that. Maybe I want more," he said quietly as he tugged on my hand.

"More what? Don't do this to me Chris." I begged and backed up before I went willingly into his strong arms.

"Don't do what? Tell you how I feel?" He stood and put his hands on my waist gently, effectively trapping me. "I want you. I want to be with you, for however long it lasts."

"'For however long it lasts'..." I laughed sarcastically. "I give up getting to know another man who I do like too, 'for a promise of however long it lasts'? I'm crazy about you already but in the long run I'm not going to get what I want. At least Derek has been married before and wants to do it again. I want to give Derek a chance. I don't know if it will work out with him, but I want to keep my options open."

"Why, if you know I'm what you want?" He argued while his hands tightened on my waist.

"But are you what I need?" I countered.

"Yes," he said with conviction.

"We've been sexing each other like crazy not even two weeks. This is probably lust. We can't build anything on lust."

"It's not just lust." Chris moved his head to kiss me and I turned my head, so his lips landed on my cheek.

I leaned back to look into his gorgeous dark brown eyes. "A woman just left here tonight, feeling angry and betrayed. Yeah, I believe she wasn't your girlfriend, but you made her feel something. Probably what I'm feeling now, that somehow I'm all that matters to you when it's not the truth."

Chris dropped his hands. "If you feel that way, I guess it's nothing more I can say... it was real."

A ton of weight landed on my heart, the instant his hands left my waist. I fought the urge to reach out to him. I searched for my purse, also tossed on the carpet. Luckily it had been zipped and everything intact. I picked it up. "I can catch an Uber. I didn't drive my car."

"I can take you home." He went to his closet and pulled out his jacket, tossed mine to me, and walked out the door, not waiting for me to go through the door. It closed in my face and I had to open it. *Nope.* I'm not riding with him, if he was going to be an asshole.

I stood back by his front door and pulled out my cell. He walked to his black Dodge Ram, unlocked his door and was about to get in until he noticed I hadn't moved. He ordered, "Simone, get in the car."

I turned away from him. "No thank you, I can get a ride."

"Get in."

"No." I found the app. "We can end it right now. There will be a car in a few minutes."

"I didn't feel like driving anyway." He slammed the car door and I moved out of his path as he stomped back inside.

I stood by his front door waiting for the Uber, fighting back tears but failing. And I was cold as fuck and though I wore a coat, I didn't bother putting it on my when I first came outside. I wanted to scream in frustration feeling like I lost my best friend that I also wanted to kill. It's so unfair. Men do this all the time. Date as many women as they want but when we do it, it's wrong. Why can't I date them both? *Because he caught feelings and deep down you know you did too.* A little voice mocked, *and Derek is safer.*

I wiped my tears. It's still the holidays and my mama will be here soon. I can just look at these two weeks as the best sex of my life and think fondly of Chris Alexander. I couldn't get sad over him. In fact, I refused, it has only been a few days. I leaned my forehead against his front door. "Then why am I so freaking sad?"

I heard the door unlock and before I could stand upright, it opened, and I fell into his arms. Chris crushed me to him and pulled me inside and shut the door, kissing me so deeply, warmth coursed through my body.

After a long tantalizing moment, he lifted his head and peered into my soul with those sexy eyes. With a husky voice, he said, "I'm sorry, Simone. I was jealous because it's not just lust. I love that you are the messiest woman I ever met. I love that you are wicked smart, that you can't dance worth shit, that you have the goofiest laugh, hell that you can even laugh at yourself. I love that you're not afraid to be yourself with me even if it means you feel like you can talk about another man to me, which is the most fucked up shit. Who tells a man you fucking about another man you want to date? But I don't want you to stop being honest with me, even if it drives me fucking insane. Every day I spend with you I love something else different about you. And to know you're going to be on a date in another city with a man who's not me, is killing me slowly."

I wanted so bad to give him what he wanted after I could hear and feel the passion, he had for me, but something in me wouldn't let me. "Chris, please un-

Chris interrupted me by unbuttoning my coat, his mouth gently sucking on my neck as he did so. "Go ahead and date him. Be warned I'm not going to play fair."

"What does that mean?" I closed my eyes as my coat dropped to the floor, loving his hands that were now under my shirt cupping my breasts, his rough palms teasing my nipples.

"I always get what I want," he said this gazing into my eyes before his tongue snaked into my mouth.

I wanted to deny or retort something smart, but his tongue filled my mouth, so I went with the flow.

Chapter 10: But this isn't dating

I spent the night with Chris again and we made love for the first time. Although our sexual episodes had been hot, sometimes quick, and full of passion, last night we really explored each other's bodies. He prolonged his own release until I had three orgasms, one from his mouth and then two from his unhurried, deep, relentless strokes. We'd acknowledged that our feelings were now involved even if we wanted different things. We'd slept entwined and were still tangled together in the sheets when we woke up. I honestly didn't want to leave his arms, but if I didn't distance myself, I would be consumed with him. So, I got up and pulled him out of bed so we could get clean. After we showered together and ate a breakfast of Lucky Charms that he prepared with the almond milk he bought just for me, and whole milk for him, we got in his truck so he could bring me home.

"You know we need to do your tree this morning."

"Why? We can just wait until tomorrow," I said looking out of the window.

"What time you need to get ready?"

"We're leaving for six. So probably four," I answered trying to speak matter of fact like I really planned to hang out with friends instead of a date.

"Okay. Then I'll make sure I'm gone by two. Unless you don't want me to come over." I felt his glance.

"You don't have to leave that soon. I wanted to spend today with you anyway. We just don't have to do the tree. We can watch a movie on Netflix or something." I smiled at him.

"No, I want to do the tree with you. The last thing I need is to look at a tree that you and another dude decorated together."

"I wouldn't decorate it with him."

"I can picture it now. He comes to pick you up, you let him in the door, he sees the bare tree and the bags of ornaments. He then tells you that you and he can do the tree. And I already know you don't think fast on your feet when it comes to lying. The next thing you know, you and he are smiling and building a moment, a moment I started. No, thank you," he said as we drove into my complex.

"I can think fast on my feet."

He smirked. "You're brilliant but lying is not you. You'll either tell him the truth about me and you or agree to let him help you. Just be thankful I'm saving you from that dilemma. Besides, I actually had fun decorating mine and you have way more stuff to put on the tree than me."

"Fine. We can do my tree though I really wanted to watch a movie." I jumped out of the truck before he did. I headed to my door, slightly annoyed that I really wanted to wait until we had the day to ourselves and not feel rushed. I could handle Derek if he asked to help me decorate.

Chris picked me up from behind, surprising me as he gave me a loud smack on my cheek sensing my irritation. I squealed and popped his arms that held me. "Put me down. You're going to drop me."

"You trust me?" He lifted me higher as I wiggled, and he carried me toward my apartment. One of my neighbors walked out of her apartment and she smiled at our antics.

"I swear if you drop me." I grabbed him quickly as he playfully removed one arm so that he held me against him with only one arm causing me to squeal even louder. "I'm going to hurt you as soon as you put me down. Stop, Chris."

"Stop pouting like a little girl then."

"I'm not pouting...okay, I am, alright...alright," I admitted when he loosened his arm like he was going to drop me.

He laughed and set me down in front of my door. "It's not going to take that long to finish your tree and then we can watch a movie. We would have all day if you didn't have a date."

"Which is why I wanted to do the tree on tomorrow."

"Not happening," he said firmly as he took the keys out of my hand and opened my door. "If you don't want to, you can always watch TV or do something else while I do it."

"No, no. We can do it together, jeez." I walked in ahead of him and I felt a sting of his palm on my ass. I turned around and hit him on his shoulder and he grinned at me. "Quit it."

We ended up having time to finish the tree *and* watched two episodes of *Orange is the New Black,* a show we both liked to watch. After the credits began to roll on the second show, he tapped my legs that were thrown over his lap. "Although that lesbian sex got me hot, I better go."

I didn't want him to leave which is irrational I know, but it's how I felt when he moved my legs and stood. I sat there watching him pick up the snacks we had and bring them to the kitchen. He already had a habit of tidying up after us whether at his place or mine. We were so comfortable with each other and we fit after such a short period of time of togetherness. Why was I insisting that I date Derek when I did indeed feel like Chris and I could really have something? Maybe I was making a big deal about needing to be married soon when he did want marriage too just not until he was more settled in his career.

"What are you doing for the rest of the day?" I asked against my better judgment.

"I'm sure I can find something to do on a Saturday night," he said. The sink water ran as he washed out our glasses and the popcorn bowl.

"Like what?" I kneeled on the sofa with my knees against the arms of it, now curious of what he would be doing while I was on my date. Last Saturday he had a date with Kat. I assumed she was the only woman he dated but he may have other women. He didn't really talk about male friends, but we had only been hanging out for a short time.

Chris's brow wrinkled as he cleaned the dishes. "We just kicking it right? I don't have to answer that."

"Why not?" I tried to act unaffected, though I was feeling

some sort of way. "You know my plans."

"And? You made it clear that you want to date others and I would only answer that question if we were exclusive."

"That's not fair. I'm honest with you."

"And I'm honest with you. You asked me a question and I answered. I never asked what you were doing tonight, you volunteered remember?"

"Well, do you have male friends?"

"Not here. Most of my friends are in the military and I have colleagues I may get a beer or something after work. But no one I consider a friend." I could see him dry and put away the dishes. "Don't worry about me. Have fun tonight in New Orleans."

"I'm not worried about you. Just curious what you were doing tonight," I answered annoyed as I turned and sat back on the sofa with my legs back on the floor.

"Enjoying myself like I'm sure you will," he said as he came back in the room.

"Fine. I won't tell you anything else about my dating life." I folded my arms.

Chris shrugged. "That's on you."

"You're right," I snapped back.

"Hey, babe, what you're wearing tonight?" He leaned against my table waiting for my response.

This was the first time he called me any type of endearment and I liked it, even though I shouldn't because I was still annoyed that he wouldn't tell me his plans. I liked it because he seemed to say it without thought and it did ease the tension that brewed between us.

"I don't have to answer your questions either."

"We already established that. But I still want to know," Chris said as he reached for his jacket on the back of one of the dining chairs.

"Why? I didn't think you would want to hear anything about my date." I wanted to answer him now, anything to stop him from leaving.

"I really don't but just curious. I want to see how you're

going to look tonight. Try it on for me."

"You really want me to try on my outfit when I can just show you?"

"Humor me."

I stood up and headed to my bedroom. "Okay. Maybe you can tell me if it looks good enough for a date walking around a park." When he remained standing by the table and did not follow me, I asked, "You're not going to watch me?"

"Hey, if I watch you get undressed, I promise your date is going to catch you in a compromising position. I'll stay out here."

I almost dared him to come with me, but I didn't want to have sex so close to my date with another man. It was enough we were so loving to one another last night that all I wanted to do was be with him much like we were this past week.

By the time I came out of my bedroom a few minutes later, he lounged on my sofa, his jacket next to him, channel surfing. He looked me up and down with a blank expression.

"Well, what you think?" I modeled my fitted bootcut jeans, and my brown sweater, and timberlands. "I figure we'll be doing a lot of walking, so I wanted to be comfortable and I'll have on a jacket most of the night since it's cold."

Chris sat back and spread his legs. "Now, put on what you would wear if I was taking you out tonight."

"Huh?"

"Dress with me in mind."

"This is what I would wear..." I stopped speaking when I realized he was right. I would so not wear this if he was taking me to New Orleans. I went back in my room and searched my closet and a few more minutes later I walked back out.

"This better?" I slowly turned around so he could see how my light blue jeans with slits in the thigh area hugged my curves, especially my ass just right, with a black sweater that dipped low to show plenty of cleavage. I wore black ankle boots that were both comfortable and sexy. I had put on large diamond hoops and shook my hair to make it look wild.

His gaze lazily traveled my body making me hot. "Yeah. You

look like you want and need to be fucked. You should wear this."

"You want me to look like this when I'm out with another man?" I asked incredulously.

"I want you to treat him like a real date because when you choose me, I don't want to hear nonsense, that you didn't give your all because you were also dating me."

"'When' and not if I choose you?" I raised an eyebrow though I loved his confidence.

Chris nodded slowly and tilted his head. "Come here."

My stomach clenched as I walked the few steps to him with no argument and stood between his legs. He leaned forward so that his mouth was level to my crotch area, and I dripped wet with anticipation of what he would do. Our eyes met before he focused on my breasts and my nipples hardened just by his stare. I kept my hands at my side at his mercy, waiting for his next move, not caring if I was indeed caught in a compromising position. He tugged on the belt loop of my jeans drawing me even closer as he kissed my mound through my jeans before he wrapped his arms around my lower back and rested his head against my stomach. I looked down in surprise and his eyes were closed.

I briefly bent down enough to kiss the top of his head and began gently rubbing the tight curls on his head. His unexpected affection moved me more than if we ended up sexing on the sofa. Chris seemed vulnerable as he held on to me and for the first time it dawned on me that I could hurt him and that maybe I was the one who needed to walk away if I couldn't give him what he wanted.

He reluctantly let me go a few minutes later and he tapped my ass so I could back up to give him room to stand. Chris picked up my hand and pulled me behind him to the door. Once there he looked down at me. "Later."

"Um...you want to get together tomorrow or something?"

"You might already have plans," Chris said with his hand on the knob.

"I don't. We can -"

You might after tonight." He interrupted as he opened the

door. "Call me if you want to hang. Take care."

He sounded so final as I watched him walk to his truck and he barely waved once he got in and drove away. I couldn't shake the feeling that he was drifting from me. And I felt powerless to stop him because I had been the one insistent that we were only dating.

Chapter 11: Scales are sometimes unbalanced

W hen I opened the door for Derek a little over two hours later, he smiled appreciatively when he saw me. He also looked good in his jeans and sweater that showed off his biceps. He hugged me and I welcomed him in as I went to get my purse and jacket. "Simone, you look hot."

I blushed, thinking of Chris's reaction before I could stop myself. "Thank you. You're not so bad yourself," I said cringing as I said it. That sounded weak, luckily, he didn't seem fazed. "Um...you want bottled water or something?"

"I try not to drink diuretics when I'm on the road."

"You're right meanwhile my dumb self just had an Arnold Palmer and probably need to stop several times before we get to New Orleans," I said as I put on my jacket

"You could never be dumb." He smiled at me. "This is a nice place. I always wondered what these apartments look like on the inside. I pass them on my way to work. Now, that I know where you live, I can stop by on my way home sometimes."

"I didn't realize that. Yeah, that would be cool. How far do you live from here?" I asked hoping he didn't live as close as Chris and that he wouldn't do what Kat did and just pop up.

"Maybe about twenty minutes away without traffic. Not far." Derek noticed my tree. "I like your tree with the LSU colors. Did you just put it up?"

"Yeah, earlier today."

"I wished you waited for me. I would have helped," he said wistfully. "Me and my ex used to put up a tree right after Thanksgiving. I guess I should put up a tree, too, but it feels weird when it's just you."

If I'd been drinking something, I would have spit everywhere. Chris was right. It was already a little strange to have Derek in my space so soon after Chris. If he insisted on doing the tree with me, I would have somehow fucked up like, Chris predicted. "I usually don't worry about a tree for the same reason but I'm glad I did. You ready to go?" I hurried him out before he invited me to help him with *his* tree.

∞∞∞

"What do you mean you don't like ice cream?" Derek asked as if I said I didn't believe in God. We walked companionably observing the beautiful Christmas lights of City Park. My cousin and her boyfriend decided to walk in a different direction so that we each had privacy since we all had been together during our travel here and at dinner. "That's like blasphemous."

I threw my empty hot chocolate cup in a nearby trash. "It makes no sense when you think about it. Why would I want to hold something so cold it needs to be in the freezer, in my mouth?"

"It's not just about the way it feels in your mouth, it's the sugar, the cream, the flavors..."

"Which I can get with fruit, cake, or candy." I walked slightly ahead. "Nope, not going to get me to change my mind."

"I bet I could." He flirted as he reached for my hand and I let him hold it. His hands were nice and large, though not as ...I shook my head slightly not wanting to think of Chris.

"I definitely could." He must have seen me shake my head and misinterpreted that I was shaking my head at him.

I let go of Derek's hand, which reminded me too much of

being with Chris and decided to tuck my arm with his and leaned on his shoulder as we continued to walk and talk. "I really love this park and all the pretty decorations. This is such a cool place. I think this will be my tradition every year."

"I hope I can be a part of that." Derek smiled down at me before he bent down and kissed me gently on my lips. He had nice lips and it was a sweet kiss, perfect for a date like this. Derek had been a gentleman and I knew he held back, allowing us to go at my pace. Thank God, because I couldn't handle two sexually intense men.

He pulled back and moved my wind-blown hair from my face with a soft smile. I looked at him wondering if I could feel for him like I did for Chris as I answered him, "Maybe. Time will tell."

"I know it might seem too soon and I don't want you to feel any pressure. Do you have plans for New Year's Eve? My boss is throwing a big bash, fireworks and all. Tam will be there too."

"Oh...I might have plans...um...not sure I might be going...going to D.C." I can't believe that Chris had been right again. I couldn't lie worth crap, so I needed to tell some version of the truth. I cleared my throat. "What I'm trying to say is I'm not sure yet if I will be doing anything, or if I'm going home. Can I let you know closer to that time?" Truth be told, I didn't want to make plans without knowing what Chris wanted to do. I wished I could really let it flow and go with the man who asked first, but I knew deep down if I made plans with Derek and Chris wanted me to be with him on that special night, I would be miserable.

Derek frowned. "Simone, look, I like you and hope that we can continue to spend time together. If you don't feel the same, we're still good."

"I'm sorry, it's not that. It's just a big night and it means something special to spend that evening with someone at least to me. I do like you and just not sure if we're at that point yet."

He placed his hands in his pockets. "It doesn't have to be that deep. It's a work party and I invited you."

"On New Year's Eve," I reminded him as we began walking again. "I'm not saying 'no', just I need to get back with you if that's okay?"

"Okay, then that means we need to spend more time together between now and then so I can convince you." He smiled. "Like you want to go to movies tomorrow? You can even choose the movie."

I immediately thought of wanting to be with Chris tomorrow and realized that I wasn't given Derek my all as Chris suggested I do. "Yeah, sounds good."

"We need to meet back up with Sam and Tam."

I giggled hearing their names said together again. "I don't know why that's funny to me."

"It is, right?" He asked and this time I reached for his hand, which he gladly gave me with a wink, and a smile.

As we strolled to catch up with my cousin, I wondered again for the umpteenth time what and who Chris was doing. And if he would even respond to my call or text whenever I contacted him again.

When we got back to Baton Rouge, Derek walked me to my door. "Can I come in?"

"Next time." I reached up to kiss him lightly, but he pulled me into him and used his tongue this time and I wrapped my arms around his neck letting myself enjoy the kiss.

"Come on, let's go inside," he whispered against my lips and that stopped whatever sexual stirrings cold.

"Not tonight. It's too soon." I moved my hands to his chest, preventing him from kissing me again like I knew he wanted to do.

"Really? We had a good time tonight and I thought we were feeling each other." He looked annoyed.

I tapped my hands on his chest. "I need to go slow, okay? I hope we're still on for the movies tomorrow night?"

Derek's face relaxed and he pulled my hands to his mouth to kiss them. "Okay. Tomorrow. About four. And we can grab a bite to eat afterwards."

"Yeah, that works," I said, now understanding why Chris refused to make plans with me. He wanted me to decide with whom

I'd rather spend time. I wanted him, but I couldn't emotionally afford to give him all my attention.

Derek headed back to his car with a smile.

"Derek, I did have fun tonight," I called after him. And I didn't feel like somehow it was over because he didn't get what he wanted, unlike Chris. That should have made me favor Derek more, but I still missed Chris and wished I shared such a romantic night in New Orleans with him.

I opened the door thinking about Derek's kiss and everything that happened tonight. I still did not feel the sparks that Chris evoked, but there was something there. He was handsome, confident in himself without being arrogant, wasn't threatened by my degree, liked his job, treated me well on dates, and seemed like a family man. I had been comfortable around him and I could spend more time with Derek, getting to know him better without the sex that seemed to consume Chris and me. Eventually Derek would pressure me to have sex and I knew that I would have to stop seeing Chris if I decided to have sex with him. There was no way I could be intimate with two men. I wasn't that free with my body and I had no intentions of changing that about me.

Bea had no such qualms and would probably encourage me to do so. She would ask how could I make an informed decision between the two men without having sex with both? And on one level she was right. I could leave Chris alone and focus solely on Derek and realize that the sex is good, or worse just okay, but have a man on the same path regarding commitment. Or I could stop seeing Derek and just be a girlfriend with Chris until he decided to move on to focus on his career. I should at least stop having sex with Chris so I could honestly compare how I feel about both without the physical. *Who am I fooling?* Just the thought of how he looked at me tonight when I modeled for him like he had to have me, and I knew I couldn't deny him sexually. With Chris, it was all or none. How did dating two men become more complicated than fun?

I took off my jacket and sat on my sofa watching the twinkling lights of my tree and then looked at the neatness of my apartment. All because of Chris. He made my apartment warm and cozy. No matter what, I wouldn't regret spending time with him, and he deserved a chance even if he wasn't ready for marriage. If Chris wasn't done with me after tonight, I would date both for now and whoever I spent New Year's Eve would be the only one I date going into the new year.

Feeling pretty good about my decision, I took my cell out of my jacket pocket that I turned off as soon as I got in Derek's car. I'd been tempted to constantly check for texts from Chris. My heart fluttered when I saw I had two messages from Chris.

To answer your question, I'll be at home watching the Lakers and Spurs and then crashing. You wore me out last night. �� *6:32 pm*

I smiled wide and hugged my cell against my chest, but it was the next message that left me floating to bed.

Spend New Year's Eve with me. I want to end and begin a new year with you. 9:03 pm

Chapter 12: Truth be told

"**B**ea, you up?" I laid in my bed, hoping she wouldn't kill me for waking her up or worse interrupt her while she was with a man.

"If I am answering the phone, what do you think?" She sounded sleepy.

"Don't be a smart ass."

"Don't ask stupid questions...but I'm tired and it's what, midnight there and if you're calling me, Derek didn't get any."

"No, though he tried."

"Of course, he would, you've been out with him a few times now. I'm surprised he hasn't tried anything sooner. If Chris wasn't in the picture you might have given him some by now."

"Maybe. You know it takes me a while to have sex even if I really like you. I get too emotionally attached to just have sex, so I have to be cautious."

"Which you weren't with Chris at all... I mean do you even like Derek?"

"I do. I would give him more time if I wasn't craving Chris every moment."

"Ooh, that dick must be good."

"Yes, Lord. It's so good and he told me he had real feelings for me last night even after he knew about my date with Derek."

"You told him you had a date and he still wants to see you? You got him sprung."

"I should have lied. But I had to say something only because we spent yesterday together buying Christmas trees to decorate for both our places and he wanted to hang out today too."

"Damn...you're doing real couple stuff. It had to be his idea. I know you."

"And you also know I'm not good with lying."

"Nope. You start to stutter and shit."

"So, I had to tell him. I could tell he was bothered but then he seemed to take it in stride and sees it as a challenge to get me to want only him. And check this out. He sent me a text tonight saying he wants to spend New Year's Eve with me and that he wants to end and begin a new year with me. You think he's serious or just trying to compete with Derek?"

"Men can be predictable but then they do things that make absolutely no fucking sense. He might be trying to get an edge over Derek, or he could be sincere. Was he upset or just bothered when you told him about your date?"

"He was pissed, and we got into...shit. I can't believe I forgot to tell you, the woman he's dating or was dating, the one he was with when I saw him at the restaurant, stopped by his apartment while I was there."

"What?" She screamed. "You can't fight worth shit either."

"How can you say that? I have never been in a fight."

Bea spoke quickly, "Which is why I can say that. You would have to be in a rage to win and in this scenario, she would be the woman in rage. Did it get ugly? He must have gotten in between you. If you're talking to me, then she didn't scratch your face up."

"Bea...Bea...chill. Nothing happened...well, it did but between them. I was in his bedroom. She cursed him out and threw stuff around and he grabbed her before she came after me."

"Was she his girlfriend?"

"No, but she was attached to him, like I am. He had been dating her for a while and if he treated her like he does me, I understand her craziness. He demands attention when you're with him but it's more his presence than something he expects. He makes you feel protected that somehow nothing will happen at least not on his watch. I thought it was just sex, but I feel warm whenever he's near. These past few days have been like the start of the best relationship I've ever had."

"Then what's the issue? You don't speak the same about

Derek."

"I feel more for Chris, maybe because he sexed me first. He told me that he wants to be married someday but there are things he wants to have more established with his career before he does."

"Some men say that as an excuse. You think it's an excuse?"

"I know that because I've heard it before too. And you and I have both felt that way as well, not wanting a man to get in the way of our dreams. But I believe him. He used to be in the military and now he wants to get an MBA. Eventually he plans to start his own charter plane company since he's a pilot."

"You're dating a real live 'Black Top Gun'. I bet he looks good in uniform. Why are you still seeing Derek again? And if it's because Tam set it up, I swear I will slap you through the phone."

"Did you hear what I said? Chris doesn't want to be married anytime soon."

Bea groaned. "Here we go. You and this marriage thing. I thought you were trying to be different this time."

"I am."

"No, you're not. You should be dating for the experience and if you find that you really want to be with someone, and he feels the same then you stop seeing everyone else. It seems to me you're only dating Derek because he may see marriage in his future sooner than Chris. But what if Chris is the 'one'?"

"I thought you didn't believe in the 'one'."

"I don't but you do. My point is you're not giving dating a chance. You're so focused on which roads lead to marriage, are you even focused on the actual person? I mean what's the point of being married if you married the wrong one."

"But if I know it's what I want then why I should date someone who doesn't want that?"

"Chris does but he wants to finish his goals first, which is something you already did, so you should understand where he's coming from."

"I do, which is why I can't put all my eggs in the basket with him. I'm ready to be married and have my own family now."

"So am I, but it happens when it happens. There are plenty

of single women much older than us, who want to be married. Life has no guarantee we'll find that special person anytime soon."

"Exactly, so I can't afford to hold on to a man who's not on the same page as me."

"You're missing my point. I didn't say that to scare you into settling for the first man who wants to marry you. I simply said that to remind you that just because you want it to happen now, it may not. And if you're not okay with that, you'll make bad choices. Life is about enjoying the ride. For once focus on the man and not the future. All we have and can depend on is the present."

"That's not how I operate."

"And you drove Akil away because of it," she muttered.

"That's a low blow and you know it," I said feeling the twinge of regret when I thought of my ex. We broke up almost two years ago because he wasn't ready to get married after we'd been in a relationship about that long.

"I'm not your friend if I'm not real with you. Akil loved you but you were focused on marriage from the very beginning and because he loved you, he tried to please you even if he wasn't ready."

"And that's what I'm trying to avoid. I'm not getting any younger and I can't afford to waste time."

"Do you know why he wasn't ready to marry you?" Akil was Bea's second cousin who I hadn't met until he moved to D.C. for an internship on Capitol Hill.

"Because he wasn't ready like most men I meet, except for Derek."

"It's been some time so now I can tell you what he said."

I sat up in bed. "He told you something and you kept it from me?"

"Yes, because you weren't ready to receive it and given what's happening now, it's a good time to tell you."

"Are you serious right now? You withheld information from me about Akil?"

"He's family first and remember I didn't even want you to date because I didn't want to ever get caught up between my best friend and my cousin. You both swore I would never be affected no matter what happened between the two of you. You remember?"

I sighed. "Okay. Fine. What did he say?"

"He had a ring and he kept waiting for the right moment but finally realized that you didn't really love him. You loved the idea of marriage more."

"That's not true! Of course, I loved him. It took me a long time to get over him. What do you mean he had a ring?" Beads of sweat were on my forehead.

"Yeah, he showed it to me. He was hurt when you broke up with him because he kept hoping you would see him for him and not as potential husband."

I had trouble catching my breath. "I... don't...understand. Why would he buy me a ring and not propose?"

"Monie, what did you love about Akil?"

"He was a good man, he could provide, hella smart, had ambition, supported me... handsome..." I tried to rattle off what I loved about him still in disbelief he had plans to marry me and changed his mind.

"But what about *him* made you want to marry? How did he make you feel?"

"I loved him, still do. He was good to me."

"No man wants to feel like, to the woman he loves, that he's not special to her, that any man will do as long as he wants to get married. You didn't make him feel like you wanted to marry *him*. You just wanted to be married. And everything you're saying and not saying about these two men speaks volumes."

I sat there unable to retort. *Was I so focused on marriage, I made Akil feel like he didn't matter?*

"I thought for once, when you told me you let go and had sex without thinking about it, that you were finally going to let go of the fairytale that you'll find what your parents had. And not just because you had spontaneous sex but more because you were willing to explore something that didn't necessarily lead to anything. You were just enjoying the moment and living life. You lasted a week. And now, I can tell that though this man makes you feel good, because he isn't ready to get married yet, you ready to throw him away. You're calling me right now, not to talk about Derek, who's ready for marriage, but about Chris."

"Hell, Bea. I don't know what to say or how I should be feeling about anything. You tell me the man I wanted to marry, wanted to propose and didn't because he didn't feel like I loved him. What am I supposed to do with that info? I loved him the best way I knew how." I wiped my eyes.

"Maybe you did, and he just wasn't the man for you. But can you for once judge a man on who he is and not on if he's ready for the altar?"

"I'm trying but it's hard. I thought by now I would be married." Tears sprung to my eyes. "I can't do this dating thing. It's too much. I am a one-man woman. I love commitment. It's why after a few days with Chris, I want more. I know you wish I was different, but I want to share my life with someone, and I don't want to keep waiting because he's not at that point yet. And I feel guilty the whole time I'm with Derek because I keep thinking of Chris and I'm not giving Derek a fair chance. I just need to stop dating Chris," I said the words aloud, but my heart hurt just at the thought.

"For God's sake did you hear anything *I* just said? Please stop saying I want to share my life with *someone*. That was Akil's point, anyone will do if they ready to say, 'I do'. Besides, every day you spend with anyone, you're sharing a part of your life. You're already sharing your life. These last few days with Chris have been fun right?"

I sniffed. "Yes. The best time I had in a long time with a man."

"Have you answered his text yet about spending New Year's Eve with him?"

"No. I wanted to see what you thought. Derek asked me tonight too and I told him I would let him know. I really want to be with Chris that night and I'm happy he does too."

"Then do it," Bea said impatiently.

"But..."

"No buts, spend it with him because you want to. It's not that hard. Focus on the here and now. The future will come soon enough."

I laid back against my headboard, tears trickling down my face. "You have all the answers, don't you?"

"I can help you solve your problems, but I can't seem to get my life right. I've dated several men this past year and probably won't have a date for New Year's Eve. You have two and you met these men in the past month."

"You okay?" Sometimes I forget that she wants the same things I want because she's always dating or talking to some man. "I can forget both and spend New Year's with you, kind of like *Sex and the City* movie, where Carrie...

...rushes to bring the new year in with Miranda because Carrie senses that Miranda doesn't want to be alone. I cry every time I see that scene," Bea finished. "I would love to see you, but I'll be fine. I'll find something to do or drink Cosmos and binge watch *Sex and the City* since you mentioned it. Monie, you're not mad at me about Akil are you?"

"A little but we're good. I needed to hear that. I feel like I owe him an apology if I made him feel like that."

"Just make sure Danielle is not home whenever you call him."

"Ugh, what does he see in her?"

"Yeah, she's a rebound that doesn't know it. Just giving you a head's up, but I think it would make him feel better to know that you don't blame him for the end of your relationship."

"I don't and never did. I was just disappointed that we didn't get married. I'll wait to the new year and call him at work." It would be good to hear his voice. Even though we didn't make it, I have always wished him well. And knowing that he believed I didn't really love him, hurt.

"Okay. Now I need to get my ass to sleep since unlike your heathen ass I do go to church every Sunday. Love you."

"Whatever, 'Miss Sleep with Whoever and Repent for Your

Sins on Sunday'. God and I have our own thing, and it doesn't require church...love you too."

Chapter 13: More

As soon as I woke up Sunday morning, I texted Chris that I would spend New Year's Eve with him, and he texted back shortly with a happy face. But I didn't hear anything else from him on Sunday. I went to the movies with Derek and I had a horrible time staying focused on the movie and my date. Before he could discuss dinner plans, I hurriedly complained about having a headache and needed to go home. It was the truth because I hadn't heard from Chris. I promised Derek a raincheck when he dropped me off at my apartment. He looked so disappointed but accepted my excuse. I really wasn't being fair to him and would hate if a man treated me similarly. And I kept thinking about my conversation with Bea. I *was* more attracted to his desire to be married again than who he was as a person. I would talk to him soon because he deserved to know where I stood. In the meantime, I needed to talk to Chris.

Late Wednesday night after no communication from Chris, I called him. He picked up on second ring. "Hey." He sounded happy to hear me, which confused me. I hadn't heard from him since the emoji text on Sunday.

"Hey." I said drily, waiting for an explanation.

"What's up?" Chris asked as if we spoke earlier today than on Saturday.

"What's up? Really? That's it?" His nonchalance irked the shit out of me.

"Yeah, you called me so I'm assuming you wanted something."

"You know what? Never mind." I hung up the cell. I can't deal with games.

He called back three times, but I refused to answer. *Fuck him*. I turned my ringer off, threw on my *Pink* night shirt and got in the bed. I was done with him. I guess he only asked me about New Year's out of some weird sense of competition with Derek. Once I said "yes", he disappeared. And Valentine's Day was obviously just his way of charming my panties off me. This is what I get for dating one of my students. God, I hate men. They will do and say -

I heard a banging on my door, and I knew it was Chris. I jumped up too angry to be excited and stormed to the door and swung it open.

Chris stood there, with his cell in his hand, looking like he just got out of bed in his sweats, scruffy beard and hair. "What's your problem?"

I snapped. "You were."

"Were?" He moved past me into my living area without my permission. "What the fuck are you talking about, Simone?"

"Excuse me? I didn't invite you in." I remained standing at the door with it open.

"You woke me up just to hang up in my face and I want to know your issue. And it's fucking cold outside." He put his hands in the pockets of his sweatpants, scowl in full effect. "Close the door now."

His tone left no room for argument, so I reluctantly shut the door and folded my arms. "Why did you just ghost me? You haven't called or texted me since Sunday morning when I told you I would spend New Year' Eve with you?"

Chris glared. "Have you called or texted me either? No, you haven't. You're calling me damn near in the middle of the night and hanging up on me like I did you dirty when you're the one dating other people."

"You're right I could have called you. But you've been communicating with me every day sometimes several times a day until I agreed to spend New Year's Eve with you. Now, nothing. I don't know if you're playing games."

"Games? Playing games? I think that would be you." Chris walked closer to me. "I've been working all week and the last thing I said to you was to call me if you wanted to hang. And you're right I did blow up your cell but you made it clear you want to keep everything open so you can date ol' dude. I was trying to respect that. At first, I planned to put pressure on you to be with me and then I figured, I want you to choose me willingly. You know where I stand. I want to see you every day but what good does that do if you don't."

"I'm sorry." Surprised by his sweet honesty, I touched his face. "I do want to see you every day too. I guess I was spoiled by your attention and when you didn't contact me, I thought maybe you were angry with me or simply moved on. And because I like you so much, I had knots, every time I thought of calling you first."

He covered my hand on his face with his. "How could you think that I was done? I waited months to talk to you and after being with you I'm hooked. I missed you."

I pulled his head down so that his lips were close to mine. "I missed you more."

Chris gazed into my eyes as he opened my mouth with his tongue and lifted me so that I straddled him. Just the feel of his hard dick against my panties and I needed him like yesterday. "Please say you have condoms?"

He displayed his gorgeous smile as he nodded, "I'm always prepared."

∞∞∞

"You're awake?" I faintly heard Chris as I struggled to wake up from a deep sleep. I felt his arms tighten around me bringing me even closer to him. It was still dark outside. The night chilled the air, and I snuggled closer to his warmth. "Simone?"

"I'm awake." My back was to him so he couldn't see my face. "Barely."

"A moment of honesty?" He asked.

"Always." And I meant it. I wanted to be that way with him because after his brief absence I realized how deep I felt for him and though I had no idea how long we would see each other, somehow, I hoped we would never end.

"Always? That's ironic because I've *always* wanted more with you. When I stepped to you, it wasn't just to tell you how much I wanted to have sex with you, it was because I wanted to date you. I wanted a relationship with you. But you immediately backed away after we had sex because you were my teacher. You seemed so nervous around me, though I knew you liked me, and I just wanted you to feel comfortable with me, so I agreed to just hang out.

I never wanted just sex from you. That night I saw you at Tsunami, I had already tried to put you out of my mind which was why I was out with Kat. And I know it sounds crazy but the moment I walked into the restaurant, I felt your presence before I even saw you. I wasn't going to say anything to you and a part of me hoped that you didn't even know I was there. But when you looked at me and I could tell it upset you to see me with someone else, I knew I had to try harder to be with you."

I could feel his steady heartbeat against my back as he confessed his feelings and I decided to tell him my truth. "I want to always know you, but as much as I want that I don't know if it's possible. I have wanted to be married forever. I'm the woman men run from because I'm honest about what I want. I have to be. Sometimes I think I shouldn't let that be my focus, but I can't help it. I don't know if being married will make me feel a little closer to a dad I never got to really know because it is what he valued, or I'm just this hopeless romantic in love with the idea of marriage and family. And I've been recently told that I want marriage more than the actual man I'm dating, which is something I do need to work through. "

"Then work through that with me. I want marriage and a family too."

"Yeah, but how long before you ready? You told me that you're not good with relationships. You also have your own goals to achieve and you're younger than me and I never want you to feel pressured to do something you're really not ready for." I whispered, "I could so easily be with you, just like we've been since that day in my office. You're already a comfort to me and have become a part of my life. I don't think I realized how much until I thought we were over, and I missed you as soon as you drove away the other day."

"I know. We got it bad." He chuckled. "I kept checking my phone, hoping you changed your mind about your date and hang with me. It's why I told you the truth about what I was doing. At first, I was playing games, wanting you to wonder if I had my own date and then I wanted to be truthful. There's no one else. I only want to see you. I'm not the best in relationships but I want to try with you."

I rubbed one of his strong arms that held me. "I could be your girlfriend. Yeah, we would have to be discrete at least until the summer, but I could do that. Dating students are frowned upon but regs does allow for relationships with former students after a certain length of time. I could so easily be with you, but we would get to a crossroads when it's time for you to graduate."

"Or maybe we wouldn't. LSU is on my list of schools for my MBA and I'm making connections every day with this job. I was more willing to travel because I had nothing holding me here. But if I have you, I don't mind making a life here."

"Are you seriously thinking of changing your plans after knowing me for such a short time?" I turned my head to look in his handsome face.

"All I know is that I like beginning and ending my day with you. I want to see where this goes and if it means marriage, I'm open." He looked down at me with a serious expression. "I have to go in to work today and tomorrow, and I know your mother comes in town on Sunday, but tomorrow night and Saturday is all mine."

I smiled as I smoothed his brow loving his take charge manner. "What if I have plans?"

Chris didn't smile as he moved to get on top of my naked

body and kissed my neck. "Cancel them."

"As long as we get to do this all day, you got me." I opened my legs for him and, he quickly sheathed himself and was inside of me so thick, long, and hard. "Fuck, why do you feel so good? I am so whipped."

My breasts were pressed against his chest, as Chris stroked me slowly. He whispered, "It's so much deeper than just amazing sex and you know it. Just let go and be with me. I'm not fucking anyone else and I can tell you still only fucking me... and Simone, I want it to stay that way. Do you feel me?"

"Yes, I want it to stay that way too," I moaned as we began to move faster and faster getting into a cum hard rhythm...

Chapter 14: Real love

I spent the next day shopping for Christmas and preparing for my mother's visit. I bought Chris a globe to represent his love of travel. Although I had decided to only date Chris, I wasn't yet ready to speak with Derek. He was a nice guy and a friend of my cousin and I have never been good at letting anyone down. He did text asking if I wanted to get together and I responded that we would soon, but I still had errands to run and had to prepare for my mother's visit. She would fly in on Sunday afternoon and was staying until Friday morning because she had to work the following weekend. I had been so focused on my dating life I hadn't readied myself for her visit. I had traveled home every chance I could, and this would be her first visit to Baton Rouge. My move here had been hard for the both of us since I went to college and graduate school in DC and we had never been this far apart. I missed my mama but needed to live down here to really feel like I could make it on my own. Depending on where my tenure status takes me or now that Chris was in my life, where ever I may end, eventually I wanted my mother to live near or with me.

Chris worked late on Thursday and texted me wanting to come over because he had a rough day. I told him to bring clothes but wait to get clean by my place. He arrived looking worn because there had been a fire on the ship, and he had to help evacuate people. He could not stop smiling at the prepared hot bath, with candles and jazz playing. He tried to convince me to join him, but I told him he needed to relax. All he would do is exert energy if we were naked together in my tub. I made him steak, potatoes, and salad and had it ready on the table when he finished his bath.

He told me about his day. He held my rapt attention as he talked about how today reminded him of his service days and how grateful he was out of the military. He liked to fly for fun and not in times of danger.

"I am going to get big if I keep eating like this. You can really cook." Chris settled back in the chair.

"This wasn't too much?" I asked suddenly feeling like maybe I was taking that we were embarking on a relationship together too seriously. I didn't want to run him off. I sat next to him anxiously waiting his response.

His brow furrowed. "What do you mean?"

"I made you dinner and a bath...all domestic things." I said, "I'm trying not to be so 'relationship' but it's hard because I love to care for others and when I heard the weariness in your voice, I wanted to do something to comfort you."

He pulled me into his lap, and I looped my arms around his neck. "I want you to be you around me. I want a relationship with you, too. If I don't like something, you'll know, and I expect the same from you. I needed this. Thank you." I rested my head against his chest so grateful for him and for once he didn't worry about the dishes and we went to bed together.

∞∞∞

When I got to Chris's place on Friday night, there was a red glitter note on the door with my name on it. I opened it and read:

Head to the lake and look for the lights.

"Okay." I was officially excited. He didn't tell me anything except to arrive to his house about eight and that we would have dinner. I walked around to the back of his complex that led to a man-made lake. It was a view I could see from his bedroom and living area though I had never sat on his patio. As I moved toward the lake, I heard Christmas music and to my left there was what looked like a tent covered with lights on his large patio. I walked to the entrance of the tent. "Chris?"

He stepped out with a smile. "I thought it would be cool to eat and sleep under the stars."

"You remembered?" I hugged him tight. I had told him in passing that I always wanted to go camping but never had the opportunity.

"I remember everything you tell me. I kind of have to so you know how much you mean to me." Chris seemed sad and I poked his dimple, making him smile. He held his hand out to me, "Come on in."

When I entered the tent, it was surprisingly roomy and there were even more lights and a plastic sky light at the top so we could see the stars and a mistletoe dangling (as if we needed that). There were two large sleeping bags and a portable heater. I took off my jacket and sat down on one of the sleeping bags. It was so pretty, warm, cozy, fun, and very thoughtful. "You really are amazing, you know that?"

Chris blushed as he hunched over to get our Chinese take-out dinners, that were near the heater. "I hope you like lo Mein and sesame chicken. I didn't want to mess up tonight with trying to cook for you. I wanted you to remember this night and not because of food poisoning."

"You never have to cook for me." I laughed. "I'm good on that."

We sat on our respective sleeping bags and ate in companionable silence as we enjoyed the holiday music and good food. Once we were finished eating, he put away our trash and presented graham crackers, a pack of Hershey and marshmallows. "We have to do S'mores. We can use the heater, or we can cheat and go inside and use my stove."

I clapped in delight and said without thought. "I think I love you." I quickly covered my mouth as if that could reverse what he heard. "I... mean...I love...that...you did this."

While still holding the ingredients, he calmly leaned forward across our sleeping bags to kiss me. "Well, I know I love you."

When he tried to pull back, I grabbed his chin. "You mean it? You don't think it's too soon? This is a little crazy, right?"

He closed his eyes as if deep in thought and opened them to meet mine. "A little. I didn't expect to fall for you so hard but here we are. There's so much I still need and want to say to you, but for now I just want to show you how I feel about you." Chris kissed me with those delicious lips of his while my hands were still around his face. He stopped abruptly. "Before I get caught up and forget, I want to take you somewhere for New Years' Eve so we can be open in public."

"I would like that. If we drive. Not quite ready for flying."

Chris shook his head with a grin, tossed the sugary ingredients, and moved me so I sat astride his lap. "We can drive for this trip, but I'm going to work on your fear. You can't be afraid when we have so much traveling to do. I'll have to think of things to distract you whenever we do fly." He slipped his hand in my jeggings, toying with my clit, making me move against his probing fingers. "Like make sure we're in First Class so it's only the two of us and I can keep my fingers in your panties so you can only feel passion and not fear."

My head rolled back, and I rested my hands on his shoulder just feeling the magic of his hand inside of me. "That might just work."

I felt cool air as he raised my shirt and he pushed my breasts together so he could suck on my nipples at the same time. I writhed against him, wanting him so bad, but needing to please him. I pushed his head away gently so I could pull off his shirt and began kissing and rubbing on his chest. Chris sat back as I made my way to his stomach and the light triangle of hair that led to my favorite part of him. I adjusted myself so I could lower his sweatpants and put his dick in my mouth. I heard him hiss when I made sure to deep throat him a few times before I began to stroke him fast not caring if he came in my mouth. He usually stopped me before he came because he wanted to fuck, but this time I was determined to suck him dry. Chris's hands were tangled in my hair as he pressed my mouth to him, and I grabbed the base of his dick with my hand continuing my stroke as I licked his balls. I could feel him get even harder and when he tried to pull away, I put my mouth back on him and sucked like a vacuum.

He moaned in ecstasy. "Fuck, you give good head."

I had too much in my mouth to respond and began to move up and down his length faster and faster.

"Shit, Simone, stop before I come... I want to fuck you, first." he protested but no longer tried to move from me.

I kept at it, feeling that his time neared as he bucked against my mouth and kept grabbing my head and cursing. When his breathing changed and his dick began to pulsate, I put my hand against his mouth stifling his yell as his cum shot hard in my mouth, some down my throat and the rest spilled out of my mouth. He continued to fuck my mouth until his orgasm was complete.

Chris laid back completely exhausted as if he just sexed me and when I made a big show of swallowing and licking the cum that still slowly trickled from his dick, he shook his head in wonder. "You're the amazing one."

∞∞∞

The next morning, I woke up snuggled naked on top of Chris. We ended up sharing his sleeping bag after he made love to me once he recovered. He was still asleep, and I gingerly reached for my cell to see the time. I sat up immediately after I saw several missed calls and texts from my mother and Tam. I opted to check my texts before calling.

I keep trying to call you. I will have to catch an earlier flight and arrive a day early because the weather is going to get rough here. My flight gets in for nine thirty tomorrow morning. I hope you get this message. 10:01 pm

I checked the time. It was nine fifty-five. "Shit...shit." The airport was at least thirty minutes away.

Still haven't heard from you. About to board. I hope everything is okay. I called Tam and she will pick me up. 6:25 am

"What? Is everything alright?" Chris asked rubbing his eyes.

"My mother caught an earlier flight this morning and is now probably on her way to my apartment and I'm here with you. I got to go." I searched frantically for my clothes.

He pulled on his shirt and tossed mine to me. He reached in his sleeping bag and gave me my jeggings and panties. "Let me drive you."

My cell lit up and I answered, "Hey, Mama. I'm so sorry. I just saw your messages. Where are you?"

"We were on the way to my place since we hadn't heard from you, but now we'll head that way." I could hear Tam in the background.

"You had me worried. Why didn't you answer your phone or call me?" Mama sounded worried, relieved, and angry.

I was a little girl again as I tried to explain, "Um...my phone was...I was..."

"Don't even start lying. I'll see you soon." My mother hung up.

"Shit...shit...shit." I stood up as much as I could in the tent, pulling on my bottoms.

"Let me bring you home. You're too tense," Chris said looking up at me as he tugged on his pants.

"No. Not a good idea. This is not how this was supposed to happen. I didn't plan for you to meet her like this. You don't know my mother. She can be very critical of anyone I'm dating because she is overprotective. She still sees me as her *child*. I'm going to get questioned and you already know I can't lie. It's one of the reasons I moved away from home so I could truly feel like an adult."

"You *are* an adult. Tell her what you want to tell her."

I shot him a look and he put his palms up. I threw on my

socks and put on one shoe as I limped out of the tent, holding the other shoe. I bent to kiss him quickly and hurried out, headed to my car. The next thing I knew two strong arms picked me up and cradled me to his chest. "What are you doing?"

"Crazy woman, it's freezing out here and you have on one shoe and no coat. I'm taking you home in your car and I can always uber back if you can't bring me back."

"But...

But nothing. I'm going home on Monday and won't be back until the weekend. By then your mother will be gone. She doesn't live here so don't you think she should meet me?"

"You want to meet my mother?" I stared at him, nervous that she wouldn't like him and how I would handle it if she didn't.

"Yep." Chris unlocked the doors and put me on my feet on the passenger side. He tossed my jacket to me and rushed to the other side to start the engine.

I got in, shivering now that he wasn't holding me, and put on my jacket before my other shoe. "My mother is my heart, but she can be tough."

"You're her only child. Understood. I wouldn't insist on meeting her but given what just happened...I could hear that she was upset and now you're upset. I think it might go over better if I introduced myself."

I sighed hoping he was right. I usually waited as long as possible to introduce anyone I dated to my mother. Since my father died, she had been both parents, and she was the mother with a shotgun to the men I dated. This was not the way I wanted to introduce my new boyfriend. But I couldn't help the smile on my face that Chris wanted to meet her. Maybe we did have real love.

Chapter 15: My fairytale

I t wasn't until we pulled up to my apartment the same time as my cousin, I remembered that Tam didn't know I had chosen Chris. *Just fucking great.* They parked next to us and I smiled guiltily at them both while my mother frowned. Tam had one eye brow raised when she saw Chris get out of the car and come around to open my door. Once I stood on the walkway, he went to open my mother's door.

"Good morning, Mrs. Austin. Sorry that we're meeting like this, but it's my fault she didn't hear her phone. Don't be mad at her. I'm Chris," he said when he opened the door and took her hand to help her get out of the car.

To my surprise my mother gave him a shy smile. "Good morning. It's no problem. I got the opportunity to spend some time with my niece. Have you had breakfast yet?"

"No Ma'am. I brought Simone home because she was too upset to drive, when she received your messages and your call. I'm going to make sure you get inside, and I'll go so you and she can have family time. Let me get your luggage."

Tam had popped her trunk and got out her car, giving me a withering look. I shrugged my shoulders.

Chris took out Mama's large gray suitcase and came around the car to Tam. He smiled. "You must be Tamela. Good to meet you."

Tam rolled her eyes slightly but returned his infectious smile. "I've heard about you too."

He kissed me on my cheek as he passed me and whispered, "Relax."

My mother giggled at his show of affection and Tam and

I exchanged confused glances. This was not Mama. I hugged my mother tight and she seemed fine as she let go of me and followed Chris. I waited for Tam.

"You know I'm pissed. I knew you were with him when Auntie called worried," she spoke in a low tone.

"Sorry, how was I supposed to know she would arrive in town a day earlier?"

"I would ask why your phone was off but seeing him in person and I understand." We were within earshot of my Mama and Chris, so she mouthed, "Tell me later."

As soon as we got in my apartment, Chris brought my mother's luggage to the guest room and I headed to the bathroom to quickly brush my teeth, use mouthwash, and wash my face. He came in the bathroom as I finished, to do the same thing and tapped my ass playfully. "It's all good. Chill."

"Okay, okay. She might seem nice but I'm telling you she not done with you."

Mama came out of the guest bedroom as we came out of my bedroom. "Chris, why don't you stay while Monie makes her famous blueberry pancakes?"

He looked at me. "Only if it's okay with Simone? She's been excited about your visit and I don't want to intrude."

I nodded and smiled that he thought enough to ask before agreeing. He was here now, and his presence seemed to have a calming effect on my mother who normally would have lit into me for not answering her calls or texts. I headed into the kitchen to prepare the breakfast I promised my mother I would do tomorrow. I could hear my mother asking him questions and to my delight he answered them patiently with no hint of irritation.

"I'm going to help, Monie." I had been blending the fresh blueberries in the batter when I heard Tam and I groaned knowing she only wanted to be alone with me to grill me.

"So, are you still planning on seeing Derek?" She whispered as she reached for pans.

"No. Chris and I just decided to be exclusive on Thursday." I poured a dash of vanilla extract. "I planned to call him after

Christmas."

"I thought you liked him?"

"I do but I'm falling in love with Chris." Just saying it out loud to someone else made it real and made me smile.

"You just met him."

"Technically I met him at the end of August but didn't date until now. And he feels the same too."

"Really? Are you sure? When do you plan to tell Derek?" She had her arms folded looking at me.

"Yes, I am sure. He was the one who insisted he meet Mama when I told him I needed to go this morning. And I just told you that I would let Derek know after Christmas. It won't be easy because he's a cool person, but it's not fair to him if I know I want to be with someone else. And we're not going to let this get in between me and you, okay? You're my only family here. We don't need to be mad with each other over my dating life." I prepared the batter to go into the skillet. "And please be nice to Chris. He has done nothing to you."

"I'm going to be nice to him. Kind of hard not to be nice to him with that blinding smile of his. Girl, he is fine." She bumped my shoulders with hers playfully. "I would have been fired a long time ago if I had students that look like him."

"I know right?" I laughed. "Seriously though he is the only student I even thought was attractive, but it wasn't just his looks. He is so much more than that."

"Well, he's certainly charming your mother. I'm whispering but they're in their talking up a storm and ain't paying no attention to us." She took the bacon out of the refrigerator. "I'm a little disappointed because I was looking forward to more double dating with you. We had fun."

"We still can. Just with Chris as long as you think Sam is okay with that?"

"Girl, whatever I want he will do it. He'll get along with anybody. But forgive me if I find myself staring at Chris whenever we do go out. I don't want him but Jes-us, he is gorgeous."

I looked in the living area where he and my mother were on

the sofa. They both smiled and were animated as they discussed politics, both of their favorite subject. He was indeed gorgeous with his brown skin and wide smile, and my heart warmed seeing him get along with the most important person in my life.

∞∞∞

Later as I drove him home, I held his hand. "Too bad you're leaving on Monday."

"I know. I will miss you too. Next year we'll share our holidays together, whether we're visiting your family or mine, or it's just us. Your mom is so nice. I'm glad I met her."

I squeezed his hand loving the thought that he already saw us still together a year from now *and* that he and my mother hit it off. "Well, she likes you because normally she can be kind of mean. No man is good enough for me in her eyes."

"I do have that effect on women." He grinned.

"Why are you so arrogant?" I shook my head ruefully.

"How is it arrogant when it's the truth?" Chris said matter of fact. "I'll text or call you every day and will get together as soon as I get back. Don't want you thinking I've already moved on."

"Funny. Funny. You'll be with your family and we can just text. I'll be fine until we see each other again." We were now in front of his apartment and I left the car running.

"Maybe I won't be if I don't hear your voice," he said as he kissed me with his tongue and I hungrily captured it already missing his touch. My body tingled with anticipated pleasure, and his sweats did little to hide his dick print when we both pulled away breathing hard. "Let me get inside before I'm fucking you in the backseat."

"Yeah, I'm not in the mood to be a pretzel." I drove a Volkswagen Beetle which was just right for me, but Chris needed more space.

He opened the door and reached back to kiss me again. "I

love you."

"I love you too." It really was just that simple.

Chris stood outside his front door and waved as I backed out and away, looking forward to his return and sharing my every day with him.

∞∞∞

"I really like him. I think he might be the one," Mama said as we sat together on my sofa watching Hallmark movies later that day.

My mouth opened in surprise. "Really, Mama? You think so?"

"Yes." My mother beamed.

"I noticed you weren't hard on him like you usually are."

"He was polite and respectful as soon as he introduced himself. He could also talk about something besides sports, and I could tell he cares for you. And you obviously like him, keeping your phone off all night and grinning in his face every chance you get."

I blushed although me and my mother were always open about sex.

"He cleaned this apartment, didn't he?"

I stomped my foot. "Mama, I can clean."

"Not this good. I raised you but you're have always been more like your father and he was messy. And then Chris was in the military. I know this is my first time seeing your apartment, but this place probably has never been this clean."

"Fine, he did. But why do you think he's the 'one'?" I was curious because she had never said that about any man I had dated, or at least the ones she knew.

"Just my gut. And he reminds me a little of your father."

"Why? He doesn't look like Daddy." My dad was a light-skinned thin man who probably favored Derek more, while my mother was a dark-skinned woman who tended to be on the fuller side. My complexion and body type were a perfect blend of my parents.

"No, he doesn't but he's very protective and attentive like your father and you need that in a man. He also wanted to make your house a home with that Christmas tree, which I'm also sure was his idea. That Chris is a keeper trust me. It's hard to find a man who really wants to make you happy, though it should be easy."

"Is it why you never re-married or even dated?"

"Oh, I tried to date but no one compared to your father. We really had fun and we loved each other so. I get lonely sometimes, but I know I was blessed to spend whatever time I did with your father and I also have you. I've been hard on the men in your life but when you've had a good husband like your father was to me, you don't want your daughter just being with any old man. And that Chris might just be the one."

"I hope so." I looked at my mother. "Now, promise you won't judge me, but Chris used to be one of my students. It's how we met."

"He's your age, right?"

"Well, almost two years younger."

"Every relationship has its own meet story, and this is yours. Will it affect your job?"

"As long as we stay low key until the summer, we should be okay."

"Then no worries, Monie. Now, can we please get back to our movie?"

I looked at my mother who I admired for so long and surprised her with a hug instead of unpausing the TV. "I love you and thank you for taking care of me and for always making me believe in love."

She hugged me back. "Always. Just glad you met Chris."

And now that I had her stamp of approval, I finally started believing my fairytale of love might just come true...

∞∞∞

It was Saturday and I had not heard from Chris since yesterday morning. Although we had texted or spoke every day since I dropped him off at his place like he promised, he had not called since he returned home on Thursday. We talked for over an hour on Christmas Day which fell on a Tuesday and made plans for Friday night since my mother would be leaving that morning. But after Christmas, his communication was brief, and he would only text. When I texted about our plans for Friday, which was last night, yesterday morning, he texted back, that there was a change of plans and would explain everything soon. And to just be patient with him. This was not like him. Although I had known him a short period of time, he seemed different even through texts. After several unanswered texts, I decided to stop by his place. We were still new in our relationship and there was no way I could tolerate this behavior, especially because he didn't really explain himself. He also had a job that could be dangerous, and communication was key to keep me from worrying.

I was hesitant to go to his apartment without permission but if we were supposed to be in a relationship, I now had that right. And if he had something to say, I would remind him that he hadn't responded to my texts. When I drove up, I saw his truck and my heart pounded and my stomach ached. Why wouldn't he answer my texts if he was home?

Dread came over me as I took a deep breath and got out the car unsure if I wanted to know why he hadn't responded. Was I about to be Kat? I knocked on his door and I could hear his heavy footsteps. He opened it without asking who it was and when Chris saw me, his eyes widened in surprise. He quickly stepped outside and closed the door. "Hey, Simone...please, I'm sorry for everything. Just go home and I'll come by later. I'll explain, I promise. Please know nothing has changed about us. I still want us."

His look of worry and his fast talking exacerbated my fears. "What are you saying to me? What is going on Chris?"

"Chris, who's at the door? Is it the pizza?" I heard a woman's voice before I saw her as she opened his door. She was a light brown skinned woman who looked comfortable with her scarf on her head like she just woke up and one of his Air Force T-shirts and leggings. "Who are you?"

I quickly looked at him furious. His sad gaze didn't waver from me as I responded, "It's not important anymore."

His face fell at my words. "Simone, I'm sorry...Please give me a minute."

"Look, I'm his wife and whatever you and he had is over, now that I'm back," she said with a possessive left hand on his waist so I could see her wedding ring.

Chris stepped forward to me at the pain that must have been evident on my face, though she tried to restrain him. I backed away stunned staring at him but addressing her, "You're his wife? He didn't tell me. I didn't know. If I did, I wouldn't have ever messed with him."

Chris turned to his wife and pleaded with a hint of anger. "Can you please go back inside? I need to talk to Simone."

"About what? All she needs to know is that you and she are over and I'm your wife," she said full of attitude and indignation. I didn't blame her. After all she was his wife and she *really* did have that right.

"My wife? That's what we doing now? You haven't acted like my wife in a long time. Just go back inside," he said through clenched jaws as he pushed her back into the apartment and slammed the door. I was at my car, struggling to open my door through my tears. "Get away from me Chris."

When he tried to hold me, I slapped him with all my might. Chris barely flinched as he pleaded still trying to wrap his arms around me. "Please let me explain. I need to tell you the truth. I've been trying to find the right time to tell you. I..."

"Truth? You had plenty of time to tell me you were already married. All we ever were at least I thought was honest with one another. It doesn't matter what you say now, because I'll never believe anything you ever tell me." I struggled against him as I tried to open my door. "Let me go now!"

"Please...I am married but we've been separated a long time and she showed up at my mother's house Christmas night." He grabbed my arm when I managed to open my car door. "It's over between me and her!"

"Stop lying! Chris, why is she here if it's really over? You've been acting strange over the last few days. Just admit you want her back. She's wearing your shirt and your ring... and you were about to eat pizza all hugged up together again! God, we are so so over. I can't deal with a man who fucking lies." He stood on the other side of my car door and his eyes watered and I couldn't give a fuck. "Go on back inside to her. We just started so we can just end it."

"I don't want to end it...I only want to be with you...Simone, I love you." A single tear fell down his face and for a moment my heart reacted until reality struck that he was married and couldn't possibly love me.

"I swear to God I'll slap the shit out of you again if you lie like that to me again. Love is never dishonest. Now, get the fuck out of my life." I got in the car and drove away in disbelief that my prince was actually the villain, and that my fairytale was a fucking nightmare...

Chapter 16: *Lust is not love*

I don't know how I made it home with swollen eyes from my tears. I drove around for a while when I left Chris, not wanting to go back home but my vision became too impaired to continue to drive safely. I came back to my apartment feeling so lost. I wanted to hurl the Christmas tree when I flopped down on my sofa and watched the twinkling lights as if teasing me of what could have been. Chris is married. Wow...wow...this is crazy! I can't believe this is happening right now. The one question I never asked him because I was naive to believe that if you step to someone like he did to me, you are free to do so.

I didn't pursue him, so I didn't feel the need to ask. No matter the attraction I had for him, I never would have made a move because he was my student. But when he approached me in my office and we had sex, I assumed at the very least he may have a girlfriend. I never thought that he may have a wife.

I replayed our conversations and I thought about our Hammond trip when I approached the topic of marriage. He seemed sad and uncomfortable. I thought it was because he knew it was what I wanted, and he didn't, or he simply wasn't ready to talk about marriage. Chris had been uncomfortable because he was already married and didn't know how or even want to tell me. I can't believe he did this to me! He had so many chances to say something to me before I got attached or fell in love because the hurt, I felt right now was heart wrenching. My body ached as if we had been together for a long time instead of disappointment of a brief fling.

I don't know how long I sat on the sofa crying but the sunlight had dimmed. I had to get up and do something to get my mind off Chris. I had no appetite though I only ate a bagel for breakfast. I wanted to get drunk, but it would be a disaster on an empty stomach. I closed my blinds, unplugged my tree, and turned off my lights in the front room and headed to my bedroom so I could take a hot bath and then go to sleep. I put on mellow music and got in the tub, grateful that my mother left yesterday morning and that I was on break from teaching so I could be as miserable if I needed.

"Ouch." I physically felt a pang at the thought of telling my mother the truth about Chris, that he wasn't "the one" because he was some other woman's "one". I didn't want to tell anyone anything, not even Bea. I felt like such a fool. As the suds drifted over me, I could see his face when she announced herself as his wife. Although it was obvious, he had remorse, I couldn't discern if his pained expression was because he got caught or because he knew he would lose me.

I had never dated a married man or was cheated on by a boyfriend, assuming Chris had sex with his wife since he had it with me. All my relationships ended because of differences or because we were just too young when I thought about my high school ones. My previous history with men and my undying belief I would meet a man like my father often made me naïve in relationships. Bea keeps telling me I need to let go of that fairytale that men are as good as my father and deal with them for who they are. The thing is I thought Chris had been real with me. I thought he was not yet ready for marriage because of his goals and I had been willing to be with him as is.

Then again, everything did happen so fast with us. We had sex and then we dated. Our love did seem to come out of nowhere. We secretly crushed for months and then he confessed his feelings and we had sex. After that, we were lost in emotion and each other. Maybe he didn't tell me because he didn't think we would end in a relationship and then he got scared to tell me? Or that he might have been amid a divorce and wanted it to be final before he told me? I sighed loudly as I sunk even lower in my tub.

Maybe I should have heard what he had to say or let him come over later to talk? My body tingled at the thought of seeing him and I nixed that idea of meeting with him. All that would do is confuse me more. The minute we were alone the sexual energy would get in the way and I wouldn't be able to focus on my anger and his betrayal.

I always said if a man ever lied to me about being married, I wouldn't want that man to ever touch me again and whatever attraction would be dead automatically. However, for a quick second, I saw how happy he was to see me when he opened the door before what I know now as fear, took over his features. And I was stupid to still want him because of that second. I was vulnerable right now and if he remotely touched me in a sexual manner, I would give it up and be angry at myself the minute I climaxed. No, it was best I leave him and that whole episode of lust or whatever we had in the past. I don't need to know anything except that he is married, and he was dishonest. We had only been dating briefly no matter how intense or right it felt, we would soon move past any feelings or hurt about it. He would probably work things out with his wife, and I would eventually meet my own husband. I laid in the tub until I was a prune and the water grew cold, praying I was right.

I crawled into bed and checked my cell that I turned to mute so I wouldn't drive myself crazy thinking that every notification or call was from him. I wouldn't dare turn it off anymore after what happened with my mother, so I decided to check my cell periodically just in case of emergencies. There were no messages or missed calls and the tears started anew.

When I finally woke up after a restless night of more tears and regret, I reached for my phone. My stomach hurt with the knowledge that I still didn't receive anything from Chris. He apparently agreed with me that there was nothing left to discuss once I drove away from him. I should be glad but only emptiness and loneliness prevailed that he didn't reach out to me, to fight for me or our love. I did see missed calls from Tam, and a call from Derek. He also left a text.

I haven't heard from you since Christmas and hope you are well. Thought I would ask you one more time if you want to go to the party with me, even if it is just as friends. I promise no strings attached if you decide to come with me. The party will be lit. I have fun with you and that doesn't happen very often. 8:46 pm

Seeing his text and how hard he fought for my attention, even if all I wanted was friendship, and I grew sad all over again. I threw the covers over my head and prepared to remain in my bed the rest of the weekend. Why couldn't I feel for Derek like I did for Chris? Maybe it was the sex that made me feel closer to Chris and not any true feelings? Sex can confuse things between people, and we did have a lot of very hot sex in a short period of time. At times I thought my body couldn't take much more and he would look at me a certain way and I would be ready all over again. And I did feel very optimistic about Derek and liked him after our coffee date. In retrospect, maybe I was premature in my decision to end things with Derek. Why didn't I listen to Bea who told me to just enjoy the experience and stop being so serious so soon? I was going insane with all these thoughts. I grabbed my phone and called Bea before I changed my mind.

"You're lucky I didn't go to church today. Must be trouble in paradise." She laughed into the phone.

"He's married, Bea. Chris is married," I wailed.

"Get the fuck?" Bea screamed. "How do you know? Did you cyberstalk him? Did you confront him? What happened? I can't believe this shit...you know what? I can because men are scum. I should be a lesbian but damn it I love dick too much. I -

Can you let me talk, please?" I interrupted her tirade on men which could go for hours. Bea had a love/hate relationship with men.

"Yeah, yeah...go ahead. You know how I get. It's about you, I know. So how did you find out?"

"I had no reason to 'cyberstalk' him, Bea. I trusted him. I met his wife yesterday when I stopped by unannounced because I hadn't heard from him."

"Oh shit! You, met her? Did she want to fight you too?"

"No, she just wanted it to be clear that whatever Chris and I had was over because she's back now. She had her hand around his waist, flashing her diamond ring." I rolled over on my side. "I've been crying and locked up in my apartment ever since."

"Son of a bitch, that dirty mothafucka...I hate men. Why they have to be such dogs?" Bea unlike myself had been cheated on before and she didn't trust men. "You get with them and they make you feel special and shit and then you find out they got other women. Why can't they be upfront? Most women would date a man even if he was dating other women if he was fucking honest about it. Men don't get it. We hate liars, not honest men who want to openly date others. They so afraid and fucking selfish that we're going to date someone too, so they rather act like you're the only one. That's probably why he did what he did. He lied to you because he didn't want you to date, Derek."

"I don't know why he did what he did. I didn't want to hear anything he had to say. We told each other we could be honest. I thought I could trust him which is why we even decided to get into a relationship."

"Well, just be glad that you found out now before feelings were really involved."

My eyes welled again. "Bea, he told me he loved me and that he wanted to take me on a trip for New Year's Eve and that he saw next Christmas with me. Whether he was telling the truth or not I fell in love with him too."

Bea said in a gentler tone, "I'm sorry Monie, this really sucks hard...I didn't know you loved him already. I just thought it was headed that way."

"I know. I keep telling myself it was just lust and by the time the semester starts I won't feel anything. But it was more, so much more. And right now, all I feel is pain. I haven't eaten since yesterday morning and I don't care."

"Monie, you have to take care of yourself. Tell Tam to come over or go see her. You need to be around people who care about you."

"I know that but right now I want to be miserable and get it out of my system and be done with him. The last thing I need is Tam telling me how I should have stuck with Derek. I'm okay. I'll eat when my ass gets hungry enough." I fluffed my pillow.

"Is he trying to call you?"

"Not at all. He tried to stop me at his place but once I left nothing. And the stupid part is that it upsets me more that he's silent." I threw a pillow off my bed. "I'm so angry right now. I wouldn't have stopped seeing Derek, but Chris asked me to because he wanted more. More when he fucking knew he was already married. How could he do that to me? I trusted that we were honest with each other. I believed him about Kat and thought that was it...but this pretty woman who stood next to him with her diamond platinum ring on her left finger around his waist blew my freaking mind. Where the fuck did, she even come from and where has she been?"

"That's a good question. Are you sure that's his wife? Maybe they're separated? I mean you were at his place too. She definitely doesn't live with him."

"He never denied she was his wife and he apologized to me for not telling me sooner. She looked comfortable in his Air Force shirt and flashing his ring." My temples throbbed as I relived the moment and I realized I was jealous too. That she got to not only be married but married to him. "He said they're separated, and he still wants us, but she obviously still wants him. I can't be caught up in drama and be the 'side chick', no matter how much I love him."

"No, I've been the 'side chick' and it's only fun until you really want to see him, and he can't because the 'wifey' needs him home. You don't want to share no matter how many women try to act like it's cool." She paused. "I'm still tripping that you fell in love so fast."

"Me too. I really shouldn't hurt like this. But I'm determined to be fine very soon. I can't let this linger. He's not worth it."

"What are you going to do?"

"Stay in my apartment the rest of the break and only come out when necessary until I get him completely out my system."

"One thing I can say about you is that once you're done with a man that's it. And you've only been seeing each other a little less than a month. Chalk it up to the game. I still say it's good you found out now."

"Yeah. I know. But couldn't I have found out after New Year's Eve? It's tomorrow. I haven't had a date on New Year's Eve since Akil and I broke up. Now, I'll be laying in my bed, channel surfing, and eating powdered doughnuts."

"If I didn't have to work on Tuesday, I would fly down and see you...okay, if I had the money *and* was off on Tuesday." Bea laughed because she never had money. She was a manager at Victoria's Secret but used her employee discount way too often. "Wait...I thought Derek asked you out? Just hang with him tomorrow if it's not too late."

"I don't want to be with another man so soon."

"Ain't no one saying all that, but it might help to have plans so you're not driving yourself crazy wondering what Chris and his wife are doing."

"Fuck. I forgot that. I've been so focused on just accepting he's married I haven't thought about the reality of him being married. Ugh!! I will be wondering all night what he's doing, especially because he had a trip planned for us."

"Aw Monie, this totally kicks rock. Where were you going?"

"I don't know but he said it was within driving distance. Probably New Orleans."

"You should go out with Derek. Don't waste a perfectly good date. You did like him too."

I groaned, "I know but he's not Chris."

"Maybe not but at least he's single. He's a friend of Tam, so we know he really is single."

I hugged my pillow. "Yeah. He did text me last night that we could go to the party just as friends."

"Then that's settled go out with him because you will be

angry all night if you stay home. And maybe you'll start liking him again, like, you did before Chris."

I heard a text come in while I was on the phone and I pulled the phone to look at it and it was from Chris. My heartbeat increased exponentially, and my body grew warm in that brief second of seeing his name. "Bea, he just texted me."

"What does it say?" She must have known by my tone who 'he' was.

"I'll call you back. It's more than one text."

"You better call back."

"Yeah." Already focused on the texts, I hung up.

Morning. I would say good, but I can't see it ever being a good morning without you. 10:01 am

I was trying to give you time and I know you told me to fuck off, but I can't seem to stop myself from reaching out. I know words can't express how sorry I am. Please let me come over and explain. Or let me call you if you don't want to see me. 10:02 am

Simone, I love you. I fucked up big time by not telling you the truth. She and I have been done for a long time. Please fon't give up on us. We could be so good together. 10:02 am

I meant' don't' ...damn spell check and that's not even a word... You know you still love me and want to hear what I have to say. 10:03 am

Somehow his humor through the phone got me to smile though I couldn't respond to the texts. My phone rang jarring the silence and it was Chris. I immediately sent it to voicemail. He called again and I sent it to voicemail. By the fifth time, I answered. "Please Chris, go back to your wife and just leave me alone."

"I can't. I love you." He sounded wounded. "I need to see you. Please."

I hung up before I completely melted at the sound of his deep voice. I threw the phone on the other side of the room. I flopped back down in the bed and covered my head and went back to a dreamless sleep.

Chapter 17: An informed decision

I woke up several hours later Sunday after hanging up on Chris. I picked up my phone and saw two more missed calls and another text asking me to forgive him and that he would do anything to get me to talk to him. I ignored the longing to call him and decided to reach out to Derek instead. I texted him I would go to the party, but I needed to drive myself because I would be coming from another party. A lie of course, I just didn't want to be obligated to stay the whole time or worse make excuses on why I didn't want to kiss him when he dropped me off. I finally got myself together in time for the party.

I forgot how handsome Derek was with his fresh cut, as he stood waiting outside of the party for me as we agreed. He smiled when I walked up the circular driveway. He looked genuinely happy to see me taking away some of my gloom. Maybe *this* was a good idea. I wore a dark purple turtleneck sweater dress and brown heeled boots. I wore my bob curly tonight and tried to put my best effort as if I'd dressed for Chris ironically. Although our affair was brief, I would miss the natural way he and I related. I could so easily be friends with him even if we never really got together. But he lied by omission about a huge fact and now we couldn't even be friends.

I walked up to Derek, who wore brown slacks and a cream sweater. "We're coordinated. *You* did get my memo."

"Beautiful as always." He hugged me to him and kissed my cheek. "Great minds think a lot. I'm glad you decided to come out tonight."

"Me too." Derek took my hand and we went inside the party. His boss had a huge home, perfect for a party. The living area alone easily held fifty people. For a moment, I felt like I was in the movie *House Party*, the energy was amazing. People were drinking, laughing, and partying hard. The party was hosted by a DJ, and everyone danced like it was already midnight instead of nine.

When Tam saw me with Derek, she simply raised a brow because I hadn't told her about Chris. I knew she was itching to get me alone, but I avoided her. Until she grabbed my hand while I danced solo when Derek went to speak to some of his colleagues and pulled me outside to the deck area. Luckily, I was still warm from alcohol and dancing.

"What the hell is going on? You show up holding hands with Derek. I thought you and Chris were a couple?"

"I found out he was married." I reluctantly revealed.

Tam's eyes widened. "What? I just met him and was already ready for him to be fam. Why would he want to meet your mother? That makes no sense."

"He said he's separated and still wants to be with me. But she was with him at his apartment on Saturday and she made it clear she still wants him." I folded my arms and leaned against the deck railing. "I can't date a married man even if he doesn't want his wife anymore."

"So, you dating Derek now?" Tam didn't sound happy.

"I don't know. I just didn't want to spend tonight alone."

"Don't do that to him. Derek really likes you, but you love another man. You forget I saw you with Chris." She looked up at the sky and back at me. "Monie, he's married? That's still hard to believe. He was really into you and got your Mama, *your Mama* to like him the first time she met him. If he's truly separated, then maybe you should give him another chance. Just talk to him. Sometimes divorce takes a long time especially if she's fighting it."

"I can't get caught up like that." I shook my head and sighed, "Why didn't he tell me?"

"Probably scared you wouldn't date him, which you wouldn't have. But if he doesn't want to be married to her anymore should he be alone while waiting for her to let him out of a commitment he no longer wants? You already love each other and yeah, it's fucked up he lied to you, but before you move on to the next man, make sure you're done with the one you love. Otherwise, you're not really doing anything different than what he did to you."

"What does that mean?"

"Derek doesn't know about Chris and you know he likes you. You're not telling him about Chris is probably the same reason Chris didn't tell you."

"No, it's not the same. I'm not married, and Derek and I aren't in a relationship. I just couldn't bear the thought of sitting home wondering what and who Chris was doing after we made plans tonight. I'm not trying to hurt Derek and he offered to only be my friend."

She jabbed her finger in the air. "Look, I get why you wanted to get out of the house tonight, but don't lead him on when you know you love someone else. It's not fair to Derek."

"What's not fair to me?" Derek suddenly appeared on the deck.

Tam and I both jumped. Tam said weakly, "Can you not walk so quietly next time? Makes it hard for people to talk about you behind your back."

He barely acknowledged Tam, his focus on me. "What's not fair?"

Tam gave a small smile in apology and slipped back into the party.

I turned around to face the landscaped lawn and pool in the backyard. Derek came to stand next to me. We were both quiet looking out into the night and then I felt his gaze. "I know you don't feel the same for me. Is that what Tam was talking about?"

I nodded.

"You don't think I realized that? I can tell when a woman is interested in me. I don't know what happened but ever since Tsunami you've been different towards me. I did think you liked me as much as I liked you and we were going somewhere. And then it stopped. But you really don't owe me any explanation."

I looked at him. "Yeah, I do."

Derek touched my hand that rested on the railing. "No, you don't. You've been nothing but kind to me so don't feel bad about anything. I'm a grown man and there are other women out here. We were getting to know each other, and it just didn't work. It's all good," he said with a smile though I could see a hint of sadness.

"It wasn't you."

"Simone, I know I didn't do anything wrong. You just don't like me like that or at least not yet. I meant it when I said we could be friends. You're still fun and maybe we were both putting pressure to like each other because of Tam. I'm willing to be friends if you are." He tapped my shoulder to his. "In fact, there's this dude in this party who's trying so bad to get your attention."

"Ugh, you mean the guy with the creases in his jeans? I thought that was your boy?" I teased.

He raised his eyes brows with a smirk. "Could never be."

"I mean who told him that it is ever cool to have sharp creases in blue jeans? I see him trying to get the courage to say something to me, though he clearly sees that I came here tonight with you. That old man bold."

"I'm saying." He laughed and it was such a strong, hearty laugh. I couldn't help but think how I should have made a different choice.

"Derek, you good peeps. You know that?" I tapped his shoulder back.

He held his arm up for me to hold onto. "I know. So are you, Ms. Austin."

And we went back into the party with a carefree manner that hadn't really existed between us. Maybe we were putting pressure on ourselves to like one another because of Tam and that maybe that was the real difference between my feelings for Derek and Chris. He and I never fully relaxed around each other and weren't our authentic selves. It was also why I felt so betrayed because Chris and I were *real* with each other. No matter that he lied by omission, what we had was real.

∞∞∞∞

As the night continued, I did my best to enjoy myself until it was after eleven and it hit me like a ton of bricks, that I could no longer be here. I needed to go because I just wanted Chris. I know it was irrational, but I couldn't help my heart. If I couldn't bring the New Year in with Chris, I wanted to be alone. I looked around the room and Derek danced with one of his female colleagues and Tam and Sam laughed together in the corner. I felt utterly helpless and alone in a room full of happiness and joy. No one paid attention to me, so I grabbed my purse and left. As soon as I got to my car, I texted Derek and Tam apologizing for leaving without saying goodbye and promised to see them in the new year.

The closer I got home miraculously the despair lifted. Maybe I needed to be away from the crowd for clarity. I have always believed that for every experience, good or bad there was a lesson to be learned. And maybe all this happened for me to wake up to the reality that I was so focused on being married, I needed to pay more attention to the man. Maybe Chris happened when it did to remind me not to settle. I thought the attraction I felt for Derek was good enough simply because he was on the relationship track like me.

Until Chris came into my life. I smiled at the thought of him. How beautiful and damn sexy he was. How he had the nerve to tell me in no uncertain terms that he wanted to fuck me in my office. How he made my house a home and made my mother smile. I loved the way he made me feel and I could only hope I meet a man again who will make me lose all inhibitions and just be. The sex was hot because he made me feel desirable and special, like a woman should feel if she's giving a man her body. And I fell in love with him because he had been caring, attentive, funny, intelligent, self-assured, ambitious, romantic, and protective of me. I felt more myself with him in the little time we shared, then with any of the men I dated in the past who I knew for much longer. My lungs finally expanded enough so I could take deep breaths and little peaks of sunshine spread throughout my body. I would find a man like him again. *Except, this time he won't be married to someone else.*

I had a skip in my step as I got out my car, suddenly ready for the New Year and headed to my door and stopped dead in my tracks at the sight of Chris standing at my doorstep with his hands in the pockets of his red hoodie.

Chapter 18: A new dawn

My heart raced a mile a minute, though I tried to pretend I didn't care. "What are you doing here? I could have had company. You can't just show up announced. We're over."

"I didn't care who was with you. It wouldn't have mattered anyway because no one makes you feel like I do." He quickly looked me up and down before focusing on my face. "Where have you been? I told you I wanted to end and bring the new year in with you."

I exploded. "Are you kidding me right now? It's not about what you want anymore. You know what? You stay right here, and I'll leave." I turned to go back to my car, not sure where I would go but needed to get far away from him. He jerked my arm. "Let my arm go now."

"I'm sorry okay? I should have said no one makes *me* feel like you do, and I would have been sadder than I'm already am if you brought someone else home. I didn't think apologizing again about what happened on Saturday would work so I tried something else. Come on, let me talk, please. You owe me that much." He pulled me into him, but I refused to turn my body toward him. We were standing a few feet from my door.

"I don't owe you shit. You lied to me."

"I know but we were beginning a relationship."

"Chris, please, please...stop talking." Just hearing him say that we were in a relationship was like a thousand needles poking my soul.

"Come on...please. Okay? If you love me like I know you do, then you do owe me a chance to explain. And after that if you're done, you're done, and I won't bother you again," he said near my ear and I felt a chill go through my body.

I couldn't look at him because I could already smell him, and he smelled so masculine and clean even though he had been standing outside for God's know how long. He picked up my hand and brought it to his heart. I resisted and he held on firmly.

"I love you. If you want to slap the shit out of me for saying it to you again, then do whatever you feel you need to do but it's not going to change how I feel. I'm crazy in love with you. Probably since that first day in class. You know I changed my work schedule to make sure I would never miss one of your classes. And I like my money."

"You didn't love me enough to tell me the truth." I kept my gaze away from him, although his never left my face. "Do you know how devastating it was to find out that you're married by *your* wife? Married...not have a girlfriend but a whole wife, a wife who still wants to be with you?"

"I loved you too much to *tell* you the truth. I was scared out of my fucking mind to tell you. I didn't want to lose you before I even had a chance with you. Why would you want to date a married man?" His voice cracked.

"If you explained that you were separated, maybe we could have figured out something. It doesn't matter anyway because she made it clear that she wants you back."

"I don't care what she wants." His hand tightened around mine. "I asked for a divorce, more than a year ago and she had been refusing to sign the papers. She shows up at Christmas giving my mother a sob story about wanting me back. I'm polite to her because I don't want to mess up my family's Christmas, but I'm pissed because that's what she does. Bring others into our relationship. I told her to leave me the fuck alone, except she shows up Thursday at my door refusing to leave until we talked. And that's all we did and maybe we needed to do that to have closure. She left yesterday morning mad because I told her the truth about loving you and no matter what, I was done with our marriage. I don't know if she will sign the papers, but I'll find a way to get a divorce. I'm so sorry I didn't tell you that I'm married."

Just hearing him say he was married was like a knife in addition to the needles in my gut, "Well, I don't care to hear about the truth now. It's too late." I looked at him briefly before trying to pull away from him again, scared in that moment of eye contact he had me again. "I don't want to hear any more."

"Simone...." Chris began to speak fast I guess recognizing his time was limited, "We married when I was twenty-one and she was twenty-five. Yeah, I know. I do like older women. She wanted to be a military wife. When I told her two years ago, I didn't want to be owned by the government anymore, she threatened to leave me. I left the military and she left me a month later. I was hurt and I moved here for a fresh start. I didn't expect to fall in love with you and didn't know how to tell you I was already married. I believe in marriage and want to do it again with the right woman. And I hope it's you. That day when we were in Hammond, I wanted to tell you. But I chickened out because I knew by then you would be angry with me and wouldn't want to date me, especially when you had another option."

I closed my eyes and listened to my gut before opening them. I finally had the courage to fully look him in his face. He looked worn and needed a shave. Chris tugged on my hand that he still held feeling my body relax, sensing I was more receptive to what he had to say to me. "Let's go inside and really talk. I need you to believe me and know I wouldn't hurt you like that ever again."

Emotionally spent, I let him lead me back to my apartment door and I even gave him my keys. But when he fumbled trying to find the right key, something in me closed back up again. I wrapped my arms around his waist and prevented his hand from turning the key. I rested my head on his strong back, closed my eyes and inhaled his scent deeply trying to remember everything I could about him. "You can't come inside. It's over."

Chris leaned his head against my door. "How can you say that? I wish like fuck I told you the first time you spent the night with me. But I was already hooked, and I know it was selfish, but..."

I hugged him to me, tears falling as I heard fireworks exploding all around me. "You're a married man. Marriages have ups and downs and right now you and your wife might be in a valley. She hasn't signed the papers and you wanted a divorce only because she left you first. Now, she's back and I can't come between that. If you were my husband, I would hope that if I did something as stupid as leave you, that you could forgive me if I came back to you begging for another chance. I'm already madly in love with you, but I can walk away, broken heart and all because I'm not your wife."

"I only want you." He turned around angry and grabbed me to him and began to kiss me. I opened my mouth to him relishing his kiss, his love that he desperately tried to show me through his lips.

When we finally broke away from the kiss, chests heaving, I took the keys out of his hand. "Thank you for everything. For showing...teaching me about love and what I want in a man. Happy New Year, Chris."

Chris kept shaking his head. "Simone...I... don't..." His hands fell by his side. "Shit..."

I opened the door, went inside, and closed the door on him. I didn't even make it to the sofa before I collapsed on the carpet and cried myself to sleep, trying hard to refrain from going after him. I could feel his truth. But no matter, what he was married and if he was honest, I wouldn't have ever dated him. And we wouldn't have fallen in love.

∞∞∞∞

I woke up the next morning still in the middle of the floor and I stood up slowly, hung over from champagne and a love that could never be. I stretched and went to the window to open the blinds for the sunlight, hoping that the light of day would make me feel better. I looked out into the sky, asking for the peace that

I had last night on my way home, when I felt hopeful about my future that I would again meet someone who made me feel like Chris. As my gaze dropped, I caught a glimpse of a familiar truck and once again, my heart stopped. "What is he doing here?"

I hurried to the door, unlocked it, and stepped into the cool, crisp morning. He sat next to my door, with his knees raised so he could rest his head. "Were you here all night? Why?"

He squinted up at me with bloodshot and slightly swollen eyes. "I wanted to start the new year with you because I love only you. You are my future and she is my past. And it doesn't matter if you don't want to be with me anymore, just knowing that you loved me even for a little while is already the best part of my new year. I couldn't leave without you knowing that."

My heart...my heart. Tears sprang to my eyes and I scooted down next to him. "I don't know, Chris."

He gave me a slight grin, "Well, I do know."

I looked down studying my hand on the concrete between us, trying to wrap my head about what was right for me to do. I took a deep breath wondering if I could take another chance on him. At that moment, Chris hesitantly placed his hand on top of mine and the moment he touched me I knew. I turned my hand in his and entwined our fingers together and looked at him, unsure of anything except I loved him. He smiled wider confidence back. "Happy New Year, Simone."

"Happy New Year, Chris." I smiled with unshed tears.

He pulled me nearer and let go of my hand so he could put his arm around me. I closed my eyes, put my hand on his heart, and rested my head on his shoulder. He kissed my forehead, and we sat together as peace drifted between us...

Discussion Questions

1. Each woman in the story approached dating differently. Do you think there is a right or wrong way to fall in love?
2. Do you think it's possible to fall in love in such a short period of time?
3. Do you think Chris and Simone were in lust or love? How do you know the difference?
4. Do you think that there was anything wrong with Simone openly asking for what she wanted regarding marriage?
5. Why do you think women feel more pressured to be married than men?
6. Many of you may have been shocked to know Chris was married. Is there ever a justification for dating a married man?
7. Do you think that Simone should have stayed true to her decision to end things with Chris?
8. Do you think Chris was telling the truth about his marriage and why he didn't tell Simone?
9. Do you think she should have given or should give Derrick a chance? Why or why not?
10. Is chemistry important when dating?

Thank you for reading my story!!!��❤❤��❤❤

Thank you for reading! If you enjoyed Simone's and Chris's story, please write a review and let others know so they can discover this story!

Follow me and/or join my newsletter, Love Notes, to learn about my other releases on my website...

Tiye Love

Also available by Tiye Love

Endgame

Game Time

Game Changer

Forbidden

Forbidden Secrets

Forbidden Hearts

One Week

About the Author

Tiye Love recalled reading romance ever since she was a young child and would sneak and read the Western love stories, her grandmother kept on her bedside table. Although she didn't understand half of the words she read at the time, something about those books captured her attention and as she grew older, her love of romance expanded to other genres and she became a fan of anything remotely related to reading and book such as libraries, bookstores, and the coffeeshop around the corner.

She loves to travel and has lived in several cities, including New Orleans, Washington D.C. and Houston and finds inspiration for her stories from every place she has had the fortune to visit or inhabit. When Tiye is not obsessed with her latest characters, she spends time with herself, family and friends doing whatever she can to create her best life possible.

http://www.tiyelovebooks.com

Instagram: @tiye28always

Email address: tiye28always@gmail.com

CPSIA information can be obtained
at www.ICGtesting.com
Printed in the USA
LVHW111700290819
629406LV00003B/412/P